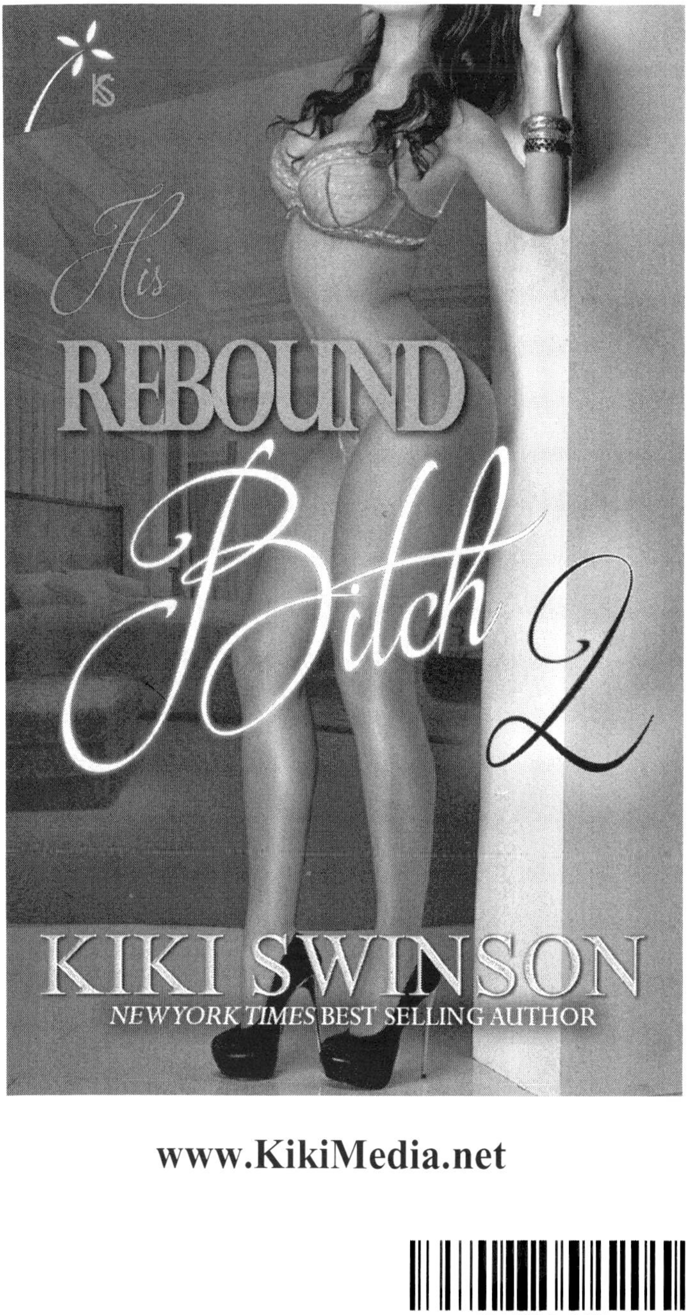

His REBOUND Bitch 2

KIKI SWINSON

NEW YORK TIMES BEST SELLING AUTHOR

www.KikiMedia.net

This is a work of fiction. All of the characters, organizations, and events portrayed in this novel are either products of the author's imagination or are used fictitiously.

Publisher's address:

K.S. Publications
P.O. Box 68878
Virginia Beach, VA 23471

Website: www.KikiMedia.net
Email: KS.publications@yahoo.com
Instagram.com/AuthorKikiSwinson
Twitter.com/AuthorKikiSwinson
Facebook.com/KikiSwinson

ISBN-13: 978-0986203787
ISBN-10: 0986203785

First Edition: October 2019

10 9 8 7 6 5 4 3 2 1

Editors: Letitia Carrington
Interior & Cover Design: Davida Baldwin (OddBalldsgn.com)
Cover Photo: Davida Baldwin

Printed in the United States of America

Don't Miss Out On These Other Titles:

Wifey
I'm Still Wifey
Life After Wifey
Still Wifey Material
Wifey 4-Life
Wife Extraordinaire
Wife Extraordinaire Returns #2
Wife Extraordinaire Reloaded #3
Who's Wife Extraordinaire Now #4
Wifey's Next Hustle
Wifey's Next Deadly Hustle #2
Wifey's Next Come Up #3
Wifey's Next Twisted Fate #4
The Candy Shop 1 - 2
A Sticky Situation
Sleeping with the Enemy (with Wahida Clark)
Heist (with De'nesha Diamond)
LifeStyles of the Rich and Shameless (with Noire)
A Gangster and a Gentleman (with De'nesha Diamond)
Playing Dirty #1
Notorious #2
New York's Finest #1
Internationally Known (New York Finest #2)
I'm Forever New York's Finest #3
Cheaper to Keep Her part #1 - #5
His Rebound Bitch #1
The Score part 1
The Mark part 2
Schemes
Most Wanted (with Nikki Turner)
Green Eye Bandit part 1 - 2
Ericka Kane

Making the Call

What the fuck is going on? William cannot be awake. He cannot be conscious. This is not how things are supposed to be. He is supposed to be dead! His wife is supposed to be planning his funeral, not getting him in a comfortable position to talk to the cops. That can't happen.

I stood in the middle of my bedroom floor with my cellphone in hand and immediately dialed my hitman's number. My gut feeling told me that he wasn't going to answer my call, but I thank God he did. "Yeah," he uttered; his words were barely audible.

"We need to talk." I didn't hesitate to say. On the other hand, I wanted to call him a dumbass since he's never given me his real name. The only name this asshole told me to address him as was Hitman, so I figured Dumbass wouldn't be that far off.

"I'm gonna call you back on a secured line."

"Please do," I said and then the line went dead.

A second later my cell phone rang. I answered it on the first ring. "William's awake," I started off, "and the cops are on their way up there to talk to him right now." I panicked. I was on the verge of having a nervous breakdown, thinking about what William could possibly say to the cops about his attacker.

"I wish you would calm down. I told you I'm gonna handle it." He assured me. But the tone of his voice gave me the impression that he was becoming aggravated. I, on the other hand, couldn't care less. My life and freedom were on the line so he could keep his feelings to himself.

"Well, hurry up and do it because now I've got to go back up to the hospital and act like I'm happy that he's awake." I spat. I was pissed. And at this point, it didn't matter that he was a hitman and that I could be next on his list. I was more concerned with the cops riding my ass than the hitman hurting or killing me if it came to that.

"What time are you going?"

"In the next couple of hours. Why?"

"Because I can use you to be a distraction." He noted.

"What kind of distraction?" I wanted to know. I wasn't feeling where this conversation was going.

"I want you to go to the hospital at 11:00. But at 11:30 I want you to leave because that's when I'm gonna strike and shut the place down."

"How am I being a distraction if I'm supposed to be there at 11:00 and leaving at 11:00?"

"On your way out of the hospital, I'm gonna need you to activate the fire alarm."

"What fire alarm?" I was taken aback by his statement.

"There's a fire alarm on every floor in the hospital. So, when you leave his room, walk towards the elevator, but instead of getting on it, walk by it and look for the red fire alarm switch that will be on the wall on the opposite side of the elevator. Once you see it, pull the lever down and take the staircase down to the first floor and get out of there. Don't look back because I'm gonna handle things from there. Understood?"

I swear, it felt like I had just taken a crash course on how to be an accessory to a crime. The thought of him adding me to the equation didn't sit well with me. But I paid him to carry out this hit, so I guess that means that I'm already an accessory. "Yes, I understand." I finally said. But when I look at it, my answer was forced. I mean, what else could I say? I had no other options.

"Great." He replied and then he fell silent. The line was quiet for at least 5 seconds if not more. It was an awkward silence.

"Hello," I said.

"Yes," he spoke up.

"Is that it?" I wanted to know. It felt like he had me dangling in the wind.

"Yes, that's it." He told me.

"Alright," I said and then I ended the call.

After I got off the phone with my hitman, I tossed my cell phone down on my bed and headed into the bathroom to take a shower. I required some type of physical therapy and I knew that hot water penetrating my body would do the trick, especially with everything I had going on in my head.

I only stayed in the shower for about fifteen minutes. The hot water started turning cold so that was my cue that my shower time was over. Immediately after I shut off the water and grabbed my terrycloth robe from the hook on the back of my bathroom door, I heard my cell phone ring again. Anxious about who could be calling me, I raced out of the bathroom and headed back in my bedroom. When I grabbed my cell phone from my bed and looked at the caller ID, I realized that it was Julian. I wanted to smile and beam with joy that he was calling me, but I couldn't bring myself to do it. The only thing that would get me to smile is to get a call telling me that William was dead. End of story!

"Hello," I said after I answered the call.

"Good morning," Julian responded.

"Good morning to you as well," I said, trying to sound like I was excited to hear from him.

"What were you doing?" He wanted to know.

"Just got out of the shower," I told him and then I sat down on the edge of my bed.

"I enjoyed spending time with you last night." He mentioned.

"Likewise," I replied.

"Think we could hang out for lunch today?" He asked me.

"I wish I could, but I've got to run a few errands this afternoon."

"What about tonight? Think you could squeeze in another dinner date with me?" He pressured me.

I hesitated for a moment because my first thought was to decline his offer. I wasn't in the mood to hang out with Julian when I have this William problem dangling over my head. I wouldn't be of good company to him right now.

"I'm sensing that you're about to tell me no." He added.

"It's just that…." I started off saying and then he cut me off.

"Okay, before you say no, think about how I'm gonna feel if I have to eat alone tonight." He interjected.

"I'll tell you what, I'll eat dinner with you tonight, but it will have to be after 8:00." I proposed.

"I'll take it." He replied and then he giggled. "You just don't know how happy you just made me."

"Well, I'm happy that I made you happy," I commented.

"Any idea where we could have dinner?"

"Can you cook?" I asked him.

"No. But there's a Chinese restaurant a couple of miles away from my home that has some really good shrimp fried rice."

"Shrimp fried rice is my favorite. So, there you go."

"Want me to have them throw in a couple of shrimp egg rolls?"

"Sure, why not."

"Awesome. Text me your home address and I'll see you at 8:00 p.m." I said.

"Will do." He replied and then we both ended our call.

I swear, I couldn't have gotten off that call with him fast enough. I mean, who wants to talk about eating at a time like this? I've got bigger fish to fry so I will handle that first.

Once I got dressed, I couldn't figure out where I was gonna go after I left my house. When I talked to Mariah's mother Mrs. Elaine Fisher, I told her that I was going to meet her at the hospital, but after thinking about it, I realized that going up there wouldn't be a smart thing to do. What if the cops that are on their way up to the hospital to speak with William decide that they want to talk to me? That wouldn't be a good look, especially if I give them the cold shoulder and tell them that they need to contact my attorney first. I know they will look at me like I've got something to hide. But hey, let the chips fall where they may.

Realizing that sitting around in my place would get the best of me, I grabbed my car keys and purse and heading outside to my car. Immediately after I got in my car, I drove to I-64 West and hopped on the highway, heading towards the hospital.

On the drive to the hospital, I thought about the next chick Hannah Mock, that's on my hit list.

Hannah also worked at my ex-husband's night club. She was a bottle girl. She always dressed in something provocative and personally delivered all the expensive Champagne, Tequila and Vodka to the VIP sections in the club. Not only was she fucking my ex-husband, the bitch was fucking half of the VIP niggas that came through the club and spent money. While dabbling in this promiscuous behavior, one of those street niggas gave the dumb bitch an STD, which in turn, gave it to my ex-husband and then guess what? The nigga I shared my bed with gave it to me. I swear, I felt so violated. I mean, come on…. if you're gonna cheat, don't bring that shit home. Keep it out there in the streets. Oh but no….. not my ex, he thought he was the man. Nothing could happen to him. He was invincible. But, Hannah made a fool out of him. She exposed their extracurricular activities, made my ex the laughingstock of the night club and got fired all in the same day after the shit hit the fan.

Based on the information that my private investigator gave me; Ms. Hannah no longer works in night clubs. She got a bad batch of butt injections and was forced to retire from the nightlife because now her ass looks deformed. Right now, she's sitting in a toll booth at the parking garage of the MacArthur Mall. So, I can't wait to see her face when I tell her that I know that she has fix-a-flat injected in her ass. Fucking dummy! If she would've played her cards right, then she'd be pregnant or had a baby by that idiot and would be collecting a nice child support check from him. Maybe even pushing a nice BMW or Mercedes SUV. *Some women just don't know how to use what they got to get what they want.* Isn't that what the light skin stripper chick name Ronnie said on Player's Club?

Nevertheless, she struck out at the batter's plate and she's gonna still get what's coming to her. No one is exempt from my wrath, so I'm coming for you. I don't care where you are, your days are numbered.

I seemed like as soon as I finalized my thoughts about Hannah Mock, my mind dove right back into the scope of possibilities that could be going on at the hospital. Then my mind proposed the idea of me turning my car around and going right back home. But then I figured that if I decided to go home then, I'd look like I didn't care about the severity of his brush with death and I could also come across as being a person of interest or a suspect since I was the last person to have talked to him outside his home. It wouldn't surprise me if I was already on their radar. I watch 48 Hours on ID. Homicide cops know more than they let on. And the fact that William was still alive, and talking, I knew things were about to get serious. So, I took a deep breath, exhaled and continued on my journey to the hospital. "Just relax and stay calm Kim. You got this girl." I said, trying to give myself a pep talk. I hope I get through this visit in one piece.

What a Way to Start My Day

I was a nervous wreck driving to the hospital. All I could think about was getting there by 11:00 to see William, Tammy and Mrs. Elaine and then be out of there by 11:30 so that I can set off the fire alarm. I even thought about how William would react when he saw me. And does he suspect that I had something to do with his murder hit? I've known William for years and he was a smart man. He could smell bullshit a mile away. He could see right through a person too. Never understood what Mariah saw in his narcissistic ass. I just wished that I could've spent more time with her after her divorce. I know for a fact that I could've prevented her from committing suicide.

After I parked my car in the visiting area of the parking lot, I sat in my car, dreading to go inside. That agonizing feeling of having layers of my involvement peeled away by the cops terrified me. But I'm a smart woman and I know that I have rights. So, if the cops start asking me questions then I will politely have them call my attorney.

Once I got up the gumption to get out of my car, I headed inside the hospital, walked on the elevator and took it to William's floor. As soon as the elevator door opened, I felt my legs buckling and my heart raced at an uncontrollable speed. I stood there, afraid to walk out of the elevator, so I watched the elevator door close. But right before it closed shut, a hand appeared and pushed the left door back open. When I zoomed in on the hand, I realized that it belonged to a Caucasian man. My heart skipped a beat and when he finally revealed himself, I found out that he was a hospital maintenance worker, and in turn, I was able to exhale. He smiled and said, "Are you going down?"

His question alerted me that I was supposed to get off on this floor, but because I was terrified of what I would face, I stood there frozen. I hesitated for a second and then I said, "Yes, I'm going down." I lied and then I backed up against the wall of the elevator.

The maintenance guy was mum then the entire ride down to the first floor. I didn't say a word either. I was too preoccupied about if I was going to take the elevator back up to William's floor. Immediately after the elevator door opened back up the gentleman stood there and extended his arm. "Ladies first," he said.

Once again, I was forced to decide on whether or not I was going to exit the elevator. And before I could make a gesture two uniformed police officers walked into the elevator and greeted me and the maintenance man, "Hello," they both said, one after the other.

I replied by saying, "Hello," but that wasn't enough. The gentleman that was holding the elevator door asked me once again if I was getting off the elevator and this time, I told him no. Without hesitation, he said, good day and exited the elevator. Now I was alone with both cops; plainclothes detectives I might add. My heart began to rattle at the sight of them. Although they hadn't shown any aggression towards me, I knew that they were here to speak with William and perhaps myself. But what do I say to them? Should I get my attorney on the phone now and let him know what I was about to walk into? Or should I call my hitman and tell him to abort the mission. There was no way that these cops were going to let William get iced on their watch, so should I make the call or what?

While I contemplated about whether or not to make the call, I watched both detectives create dialogue about how long their day had been and that they couldn't wait until after they finished their shift, "I'm gonna go home, get myself a cold bottle of beer, lay back in my recliner and watch the rest of the game." He boasted.

"Sounds like a nice plan to me." His partner said and a few seconds later, the elevator door opened. "Getting off?" The other cop asked me.

"Yes, thank you," I said and then I exited the elevator. I walked slowly onto the floor, dreading the walk towards William's room. I also dreaded the Q & A session I was going to have with the cops behind me. The thought of them backing me into a corner sicken me. "Lord Jesus, please be with me," I uttered quietly. Letting them hear me would be the dumbest thing I could ever do. To make sure of that, I casually turned to my right and looked over my shoulders to see the distance between us. And when I laid my eyes on them, I was shocked to see both cops walking in the opposite direction. I let out a big sigh, but I knew that I wasn't out of the woods yet. I had to face William and his wife, so I took a deep breath, exhaled and then I continued to William's room.

There was a clock on the wall of the hallway that led to William's room and it said 10:59. I was right where I was supposed to be. All I had to do now was get through this visit with William and make my exit by 11:29; I think I can manage that.

It gave me much comfort when I walked into the room and found Mrs. Elaine sitting by William's bedside. She stood up and walked midway to greet me. We embraced each other. "Thank you for coming." She said and then she stepped aside, giving me a path to walk and stand next to William's bed.

I took a total of seven steps and that left me with 2 feet between William and me. I dreaded looking into his face, but I knew I had to, or things would get awkward. "You see he's awake," Mrs. Elaine smiled like there was a glimmer of hope looming over William's head.

I slowly lifted my head as my heart raced at the speed of lightning. I couldn't think straight because I had no idea how this moment was going to go, but it had to be done, nevertheless.

Finally, William and I were staring into each other's eyes. The look on his face was that of a helpless child needing comfort from his mother. I had no idea what to say to him. "Can he talk?" I looked at Mrs. Elaine and asked.

"No, not yet. But we're feeling optimistic that he will come around in the next day or so." She replied.

"Where is his wife?" My questions continued. I tried to keep my attention focused on Mrs. Elaine as long as I could. Looking at William made me feel uncomfortable because I had something to do with his situation. If I was forced to take a polygraph test I'd fail miserably.

"She's in the bathroom." Mrs. Elaine told me as she pointed to the door that looked like a closet door on the other side of the room. Seconds later, Tammy opens that same door and comes strolling into the room.

She greets me by saying hello and then she turns her attention towards William. "Can you believe it?" She started off saying, "My baby is alive and well," she acknowledged.

"I see," I replied, hoping to sound enthusiastic.

"Prayer works." Mrs. Elaine chimed in.

"It sure does." Tammy agreed as she rubbed her hands across William's arms.

William laid there and watched all three of us standing around his bed. I thought he'd be able to nod his head or make a facial gesture, but he couldn't. Knowing this made me feel a little more at ease. I dug deep down inside of me, mustered up all the energy I had and formed a convincing smile right after I turned my attention back towards William. "It's good to see you're awake." I finally said.

He didn't reply, of course, so Tammy spoke for him. "I prayed for this day and God answered," Tammy announced.

“We all prayed for him.” Mrs. Elaine interjected.

“Wanna say something to him?” Tammy asked me. “He can hear you.” She added.

The thought of talking to William didn't sit well with me, especially around Tammy and Mrs. Elaine. I mean, I just cursed his ass out a few days ago for being an asshole and reneging on his promise to let Mrs. Elaine spend more time with the kids. And on top of that, the only reason why I'm here is because Mrs. Elaine wanted me here. Let's face it, I hate this guy. He's supposed to be dead right now. So, what could I possibly say to this guy? *Hello William, you know I don't like you. You took my best friend's kids away from her. Then you caused her to commit suicide. And because of it, I paid a hitman to kill you but he fucked the job up and now here we are; standing around your bed like we give a damn about your well-being. Truth is, Mrs. Elaine and I think you're a piece of shit. So, in short, fuck off!*

“Don’t be shy. He won’t bite.” Mrs. Elaine said with a smile.

I hesitated for a second and then I said, "William, you know the girls are missing you badly so get well soon." I swear, I wanted to grit my teeth at him, but I kept it classy.

"I've been telling him that since he opened his eyes," Tammy mentioned.

“I said it to him too.” Mrs. Elaine also mentioned.

The whole time Mrs. Elaine and Tammy spoke, William didn’t take his eyes off me. It almost felt like he was looking through me; trying to read my mind. “Can he move any part of his body?” I wanted to know.

“No,” Tammy spoke first.

“He’s not paralyzed, right?” I wondered aloud.

“No, he’s not. The doctor said that with the right amount of physical therapy, he could be back to normal again.” Tammy replied with optimism.

“Do you know how much longer he’s gonna have to be here?” My questions continued.

“No. He didn’t mention it. My main concern is that he gets the proper care so he can live a normal life again.” Tammy explained.

“What about the cops? Have they given you guys any new information or leads on his case?” I asked, hoping to gather whatever information I could so that I could stay one step ahead of the detectives.

“No, they haven’t said anything. But I called them right after William opened his eyes. They said that they're gonna stop by. So, they should be here at any moment." Tammy informed me.

"I hope they find out who did this to him and lock 'em away and throw away the keys." Mrs. Elaine interjected. I could hear the anger in her voice. And what was so weird about it, was that she was talking about me. I was the one that would be thrown in jail and had the keys thrown away. Boy, that would be a shit show, and I can't have that. Not now, not ever.

"Don't worry Mrs. Elaine, we will find out who did this to William," Tammy assured us.

While Tammy and Mrs. Elaine were creating a dialogue about William and the person behind his attack someone knocks on the door. The sudden knock caught me off guard, so I jumped a bit and turned my attention towards the door. Tammy walked over to the door and opened it and in comes a hospital kitchen staff carrying a tray of food in her hand. "I was told by the nurse that this patient was awake, so I brought a lunch just in case he gets hungry." The Caucasian female stated.

"Thank you," Tammy said and then she walked away from the door. She placed the tray of food down on the roll table next to William's bed and started inspecting it. "Looks like they gave him a bowl of chicken broth, apple juice, and Jell-O." She declared.

"That's what the hospital docs…." Mrs. Elaine started, "They start with a liquid diet and then a couple of days later, they'll gradually faze him to more solid foods like mash potatoes and oatmeal." Mrs. Elaine continued.

"Mrs. Elaine, take a load off. You've been standing up since you walked into the room." Tammy pointed out.

"I guess I have, huh? I didn't realize that. I'm so fixated on William and his progress I've forgotten all about myself." She chuckled and then she took a seat in the chair on the left side of the bed.

"Why don't you take a seat too." Tammy insisted.

"Oh no, I'm alright. I'm about to head out of here. Got some running around to do." I told her after looking at the clock on the wall. I had to be out of this hospital by 11:30 and it was 11:27 now, so I've got to go.

"I'm sorry, I hope it's nothing important," Tammy commented.

"No worries, everything is good." I tried assuring her. Whether she knew it or not, I was trying to get out of there before the cops came. I wanted no parts of any of this shit.

"Why don't you call me later and I'll fill you in on any new developments." Mrs. Elaine suggested to me.

"I think that's a good idea. I'll call you as soon as I get home and settle down." I promised her.

"Perfect." She said and then she extended her arms so that I could hug her. Immediately after I embraced her, I whispered in her ears and told her how much I loved her and not to let this situation with William consume her. Her only words were, "I won't." But I knew better. Mrs. Elaine was a beautiful person. She was the kind of woman that would take a complete stranger off the streets and allow them to live with her. That's just how kind she was. But I was going to look after her. William's miserable ass didn't deserve to have Mrs. Elaine in his corner. He was a piece of shit and I will continue to remind her of that.

After I released Mrs. Elaine from my hug, I walked around the bed and gave Tammy one of those *pat you on your back* hugs. Yeah, the fake and phony hugs and then I told her to call me if she needed anything. She assured me that she would, but I knew she was lying. And I could care less.

On my way out of the room, I waved at William and told him to get well and then I blew a kiss at Mrs. Elaine. And as soon as I walked out of the room and closed the door behind me, it felt like a ton of bricks had been lifted off my shoulders. What a great feeling that was.

Sticking to the Script

Free and clear of that black cloud looming inside William's room, I headed towards the elevator so I could get the hell out of this hospital. Midway to the elevator I looked at the left side of the wall and saw the fire alarm that the hitman told me about. As I walked towards, I took a quick look over my left shoulder to see if someone was standing around and when I saw that the coast was clear, I turned my attention back to the fire alarm and continued towards it. I quickly looked down at my wristwatch and saw that the time was 11:29 and that sent a shock wave of anxiety, paranoia, fear and a slew of other emotions through me and it almost caused me to get cold feet. But I knew that I had to do this. So, without giving it another thought I casually extended my arm towards the wall and pulled down the red fire alarm lever. Within seconds the fire alarm sounded off. The high pitch sound blared like a siren. At one point, I couldn't think clearly. But I knew that I had to make a run for it. Get out of there, because that's what I was instructed to do. And besides that, I couldn't let anyone see me near this thing. If they did, then they'd know that I had activated it.

With a ton of trepidation spiraling out of control inside of me, I raced to the exit door that leads to the stairs. After I pushed the door open, I took the stairs all the way down to the first floor. But by the time I got to the floor underneath me, a dozen people were already in the stairwell trying to get to the first floor like me. It felt like I was amongst a herd of cattle trying to run for their lives. It was sheer pandemonium.

"Does anyone know where the fire is?" One middle-aged black woman asked. I couldn't tell if she was an employee or a visitor.

"I heard that someone accidentally started a chemical fire on the fifth floor." A young white guy replied.

But neither one of them had the slightest clue. It's funny how rumors start. Rumors can get people killed. And in this instance, one person was about to meet their maker. I'm just glad that it wasn't me. I have a lot of life left inside of me to live. And once this whole thing ends, I will move away from this God-forsaken place and start over with a new life.

After two minutes and twenty-seven steps later, I was in the lobby of the hospital following dozens of people out the sliding front doors. It felt like I was involved in an elementary school fire grill. The only difference between then and now, I'm getting in my car and going home and I'm not looking back.

Five minutes into my drive, my cell phone rings. Startled by it, I looked down at the caller ID and noticed that Mrs. Elaine was calling me. I was afraid to answer my phone, but I knew that I had to, especially after the fire alarm chaos I started back at the hospital. “Hello,” I said after answering the call on the third ring. Before Mrs. Elaine uttered a word the blaring sound of the fire alarm struck my eardrums. The sound was unbearable. It was ear-piercing.

"Hey, where are you?" She yelled over the background noise.

"On my way home," I yelled back. I wanted her to hear what I was saying. "And what is all that noise?" I added. I wanted her to think that I didn't know what was going on.

"It's the fire alarm. They're making us evacuate the hospital." She yelled.

“Where is Tammy?”

"She's in the hallway somewhere trying to find out if hospital staff is going to move William." She tried desperately to say above all the noise. "Hey Kim, let me call you right back. Someone is here to move William's bed." She shouted and then the call ended.

My anxiety went to another level thinking about the possibility that the hitman could miss this opportunity again. "Ugh!" I snapped and started punching the steering wheel of my car. "Why can’t this guy get his shit together? It seems like every time he goes on his witch hunt; he fumbles the ball.” I roared. Thankfully my car windows were rolled up because everyone outside my car would hear my rant.

Knowing what I know, I wanted to call him and ask him what the hell was he doing but I decided against it. Something inside of me told me to chill out and let the man do his job. There was no way that he could fuck the job up twice. No way. So, I'm gonna hold on to my composer until I hear something back from him or get a call back from Mrs. Elaine.

I collapsed on the sofa in my living room as soon as I walked into the house and dropped my purse on the coffee table. I needed to take the load off and unwind, especially with everything going on in my head. I hated feeling like this. I also hated being in the dark about things associated with me. Just recently, I've become *the take control* type of chick. That's one of the reasons I took control of my situation while I was married to my ex-husband and had his ass followed by my private investigator. There was no way that I was going to continue to let him dictate how our marriage was going to run. He cared less about my feelings, so I did something about it. I took what the investigator gave me and used it in court during our divorce and I got what I wanted in the end. I thought that after the judge awarded me with a nice settlement that I was going to be happy, but I wasn't; which was why I hired the hitman. Now, I feel like I'm getting my just do.

While I laid back on my sofa, I powered on the TV and started watching the Price is Right. I thought this show would take my mind off what was going on at the hospital, but it didn’t. I wanted to know what was going on. I wanted to know if William had gotten the bullet he deserved. I wanted him to suffer like my best friend Mariah suffered before she ended her life. I also wanted Tammy's miserable ass to suffer too. Feel the pain Mariah felt when William took her kids from her in that bogus ass restraining order. He treated my best friend like shit while they were married and even after they got divorced. During this deed for Mariah was nothing for me to do. I loved her like she was my sister and I loved her kids like they were mine. I would do anything for her.

An hour went back, and I hadn't heard anything. I immediately called Mrs. Elaine but she didn't answer. I even tried to call the hitman's cell phone number and he didn't answer either. Fear of the unknown crept back into my heart once again. "Where are you, Mrs. Elaine? Answer your phone." I begged out loud like she could hear me. Unfortunately for me, my call wcnt unanswered once again. But as soon as I pressed the END BUTTON my cell phone started ringing. I looked at the caller ID and noticed that it was Mrs. Elaine's cell phone number. I felt a sense of relief knowing that she was calling me back. "Mrs. Elaine, thanks for calling me back." I started off saying.

"This isn't Mrs. Fisher. This is Officer Hugo. Am I speaking with Kim?" I heard a black man say authoritatively. I swear my heart sunk into the pit of my stomach. Why the hell is a police officer answering Mrs. Elaine's cell phone? Where is she?

"Yes, yes you are." I almost hesitated to say, trying to convince myself to stay calm.

"Kim, what's your last name?" He questioned me again.

"Weeks. My name is Kim Weeks."

"What's your relationship with Mrs. Fisher?" He wanted to know.

"She's the mother of my best friend. I'm like a daughter to her." I replied. "Is there something wrong?" I turned the questions back to him.

"I can't say right now. But, is there a way I can get in contact with a next of kin?" He wanted to know.

"She has family in Delaware and North Carolina. But I don't have a number to contact them." I told him. "Look, is there something wrong?" I pressed the issue.

"I'm not at liberty to say at the moment."

"Where is Tammy? Let me speak to her." I demanded. This cop was getting on my fucking nerves. I needed answers and he wasn't giving them to me.

"She's speaking with another officer. So, give her a few minutes and then give her a call." He suggested.

"But I don't know her cell phone number."

"I'm sorry but I don't know what else to tell you." He said nonchalantly.

I let out a long sigh and then I said, "Yeah, whatever." I ended my call with him a second later. As soon as I freed the line, I called the hitman again. The phone rang five times and then it went to voicemail again. I cleared the line again and then I called him back once more. This time I got six rings before it went to voicemail. I sucked my teeth. I was getting aggravated by the minute. "Answer your freaking phone," I said. I was boiling on the inside now.

Instead of trying to get him on the line for the fourth time I stood up from the sofa, slipped my shoes back on my feet, grabbed my purse and car keys from the coffee table and scurried out of my house. Filled with a load of emotions I was given only one option and that was going back up to the hospital.

I was a nervous wreck during my drive back to the hospital. All sorts of things ran through my mind. Things like being in the dark about what was going on at the hospital were one of them. Not being able to speak with Mrs. Elaine and the hitman was another. I needed some answers but for some reason, I kept hitting a brick wall. In due time, though.

Watching My Back

I drove at a speed of 60 mph. in a 45-speed zone all the way to the hospital. When I pulled in the parking lot of the front entrance, cop calls were all over the place. Spooked by the number of cars in front of me, I almost put my car in reverse, turned around and took my ass back home. But that wouldn't have been a good idea. I had to show my face. Act surprised. But more importantly, act like I was concerned about all parties affected by this unfortunate situation.

I exited my car and headed towards the main entrance of the hospital. Before I could get within 100 feet of the front entrance, I was stopped in my tracks by a young black-uniformed police officer. "I'm sorry ma'am, but no one is allowed to enter the hospital right now." He told me.

"I was just told to come up here," I replied, giving him the half-truth.

"Who told you to come here?" He wanted to know.

"I don't remember the officer's name but when I called the cell phone of my God-mother who's here to visit a gunshot victim named William, he answered it and told me that he couldn't give me any information over the phone and that I needed to come up to the hospital. So, here I am." I explained.

"What floor is this gunshot patient is on?"

"The fifth floor," I added.

"Give me a moment." He said and then he turned his back towards me. "This is Reid, badge number 4892, I have a woman standing next to me saying that she was told to come to the hospital because of her relationship with the gunshot victims." He continued.

After hearing this cop say the word victims, meaning there was more than one person wounded, my heart collapsed to the pit of my stomach. "Wait, did you just say victims?" I asked as I peered around to his face.

"Reid, what's your position?" I heard the other cop ask.

"At the visitor's entrance of the hospital."

"What's her name?" The other cop's questions continued.

"What is your name ma'am?" He turned back around to face me.

"Kim. Kim Weeks." I answered him. And immediately after I uttered my name from my mouth, it felt like I had exposed myself and let the whole world know that I was here. It was a weird feeling.

"She said her name was Kim Weeks." The officer next to me said.

"Okay, wait, Hugo talked to her. Could you escort her up to the fifth floor?" He replied.

"Ten-four," the cop next to me said and then he instructed me to follow him.

I swear, my first step felt like I was moving a brick. I did not want to go upstairs after hearing the word victims. I wanted to send a quick prayer up to God, but I knew He wouldn't be trying to hear from me. Not after I put a bounty on William's head.

"So, what happened?" I started asking the cop questions after he and I got onto the elevator.

"I'm gonna let the Sergeant tell you." He insisted.

"Well, could you at least tell me if someone is dead?" I probed him more. I needed some damn answers. I don't like being in the dark about anything.

"I can't say. Sergeant Miles or Officer Hugo will be able to answer all of your questions after we get upstairs." He explained.

I swear, I wasn't feeling this nigga at all. I mean, why not tell me.? You already insinuated that there were victims involved. Why not let the cat out of the bag? I mean, it's not like I won't find out what happened.

The elevator ride up to the fifth floor took less than a minute and a half. So, immediately after the door opened, a uniformed cop was standing there awaiting my arrival. "She's all yours," Officer Reid said as if he was handing me over to this cop standing in front of the elevator.

After I stepped off the elevator the cop extended his hand and introduced himself. "Mrs.

Weeks, I’m Officer Hugo,” he said as he shook my hand.

"Hi," I replied because I didn't know what to say to him.

"Follow me this way." He instructed me. He started walking towards William's room and I followed. The second I started taking steps in that direction I saw yellow crime tape roped off around William's room. My heart skipped a beat and that's when I knew that the hitman had finished what he started and that was end William's life. But when I saw Tammy sitting on a chair down the opposite direction of the hallway, her face in her hands, I realized that she hadn't gotten crossed up in the hitman's line of fire.

"Kim Weeks, this is Sergeant Miles, he will be answering all your questions from here." Officer Hugo told me after we'd taken about ten steps, stopping near the nurse's station. "Follow me to this room over here." He said while pointing to a very small room only a few feet away.

"Sure, but can you tell me what this is all about?" I said, my heart beating uncontrollably. I wanted some answers. I hate being left in the dark about shit.

“I’ll tell you as soon as we go into that room.” He assured me.

Once again, being told what to do, I put one foot in front of the other and headed into the direction of the room. As soon as we walked inside, he instructed me to take a seat in one of the three chairs that were placed around a small square desk. I sat down and said, "Look, sir, please stop tip-toeing around me and just spit it out."

Sergeant Miles closed the door to the room and then he turned around and stood there looking down at me. “Mrs. Fisher was shot twice in her abdomen area and now she‘s in surgery fighting for her life.”

Sick to my stomach, I clutched my belly like I was 7-months pregnant. "Shot?! No way. That can't be true." I replied while trying to process what he was saying. By this time, I had a ton of knots turning in a circular motion in my stomach.

“I’m afraid, it is,” he assured me.

“How did it happen? And where?” My questions continued.

When Sergeant Miles was about to answer my question, a cop dressed in plain clothes knocked on the door. Sergeant Miles turned back around and opened the door. Standing on the other side of the door was another cop. But this cop was in uniform. “Hey Sergeant, Sergeant Paine needs you down in the control room.”

“I’m in the middle of an interview. Send Detective Green.”

“Here’s busy talking to one of the nurses.” The cop replied.

Sergeant Miles shook his head back and forth and then he huffed. "Will, somebody do something without me for a change?"

The other cop shrugged his shoulders. “I’m just the messenger.” He commented.

Sergeant Miles looked back at me and said, “Will you stay here until I get back?”

I wanted to tell him *hell no*. But I did the noble thing by saying that I would. Besides, Mrs. Elaine was in surgery and I need to find out what happened.

Immediately after I gave Sergeant Miles the green light that I would be in the same spot when he returned, he left the room. Filled to the rim of guilt and anxiety, I took a deep breath and exhaled. Thinking about the possibility that the hitman could be behind Mrs. Elaine's shooting felt gut-wrenching. Please don't let this be the case. I know that I wouldn't be able to live with myself if the hitman pulled the trigger on her.

Sitting here in this room felt like the walls were closing in on me. One minute I was feeling paranoid and then the next minute I started feeling like I was starting to hyperventilate. In addition to that, the palms of my hands started sweating profusely. "Come on Kim, stay calm. You can get through this." I encourage myself.

For the first 5 minutes of being alone in this room, I looked down at my wrist-watch at least a dozen times and so I figured that if I had to be in this small box for longer than another 5 minutes, I was going to lose my damn mind. So, without further hesitation, I stood up from my seat, opened the door and walked out of the room. As soon as I walked back into the hallway, I saw a couple of cops and forensic specialists talking to each other and moving around the area of William's room. "Are you lost?" A cop walked up behind me and said.

Startled by his unexpectant appearance, I turned around and looked over my shoulder. “No, I’m not lost. I’m looking for Tammy Slone. She was just sitting down on a chair talking to a police officer down the other end of the hallway when I first got off the elevator.” I explained to him.

“And you are?” He wanted to know.

"My name is Kim Weeks. I was just sitting in that room behind you talking to Sergeant Miles. But another cop knocked on the door and told him that he was needed down in the control room. So, he left and now I am standing here talking to you." I told him.

"Well, you can't be standing here in the hallway and especially while we're processing this area. This is a crime scene." He added.

“I know this is a crime scene. And I will get out of your way as soon as you tell me where Tammy Slone is.” I said sarcastically.

“Kim, I’m over here.” I heard a woman’s voice say.

Realizing whose voice it was, I turned around in the direction it was coming from. Standing near the elevator was Tammy and her face was flushed. Her eyes were bloodshot red, her cheeks were puffy, and it looked like she was carrying the weight of the world on her shoulders. Seeing the condition, she was in, I started walking in her direction. I figured that if anyone knew what was going on, it would be her. I gave her a look of concern as I walked towards her. As soon as I got within arms reach of her, she broke down in tears and then her knees buckled. If I hadn't lean in towards her with my arms opened, she would've collapsed on the floor. "What am I going to do Kim? William is dead. His killer came back and finished him off. He even shot Mrs. Elaine and now they have her in surgery trying to save her life." Tammy belted out in my arms.

I don’t know how, but her body felt hollow in my arms. I embraced her like a mother would do a child. “It’s okay, let it out.” I coached her, allowing her to bury her face in my chest as I rubbed her back in a circular motion. But then suddenly, she pulled back from me and looked directly into my eyes.

“No, it’s not. My husband is gone. And someone is going to pay for it.” She roared.

Seeing the intensity of evil in her eyes, I knew she meant every word she just uttered. I stood there in front of her, not knowing what to say. I had no rebuttal for her. I mean, what could I say? She just loss her husband. And then the grandmother of her stepchildren was shot too. I can only pray that Mrs. Elaine comes out alive after all of this. She wasn't supposed to be hit. I only gave the hitman instructions to finish William off, not Mrs. Elaine.

I know one thing; this motherfucker sure has a lot of explaining to do. I'm gonna need a refund too.

While I stood there, trying to comfort Tammy, I heard talk over the radio from a cop standing a few feet away from us. "This is Officer Lester, we have a suspect in custody." I heard a cop say.

Hearing the words, suspect in custody nearly caused me to have a heart attack. Tammy, on the other hand, gave off an expression of relief. "Who is it?" She became more alive. A sudden wave of dread consumed me. I didn't know whether to excuse myself or stand there and act like I was rallying around Tammy and the cops.

“Lester, what is your position?” The cop near us spoke into his radio.

"On the south side of the hospital where the recycle dumpsters are." The cop replied.

"Who's with you?" The same caught asked.

“Campbell is with me.”

“Bring the suspect to the control room.” Another voice instructed and when I honed in on the voice, I knew it was Sergeant Miles talking.

“Where is the control room? I need to see this evil person that ended my husband’s life.” Tammy snapped as she stormed towards the elevator.

“No ma’am, I’m afraid that I can’t let you leave this floor.” The cop next to us informed her while he blocked her from pressing the elevator button on the wall.

"You better get out of my way before I do something that I may regret later." She threatened him.

"Ma'am, you touch me, that constitutes as assault. And I really don't want to arrest you, especially after losing your husband." He warned her.

"Yeah, Tammy, let's not do that. Let them handle it. I'm sure they'll let you see whoever they have in custody when the timing is right." I said, siding with the cop.

"But what if he gets away?" She pressed the issue.

"Ma'am, trust me that whoever they have in custody will not go anywhere." The cop guaranteed her.

She stood there with a clueless expression on her face. "So, what do I do now?" She wanted to know.

"Come on with me," I interjected, not knowing where to take her. The whole floor seemed like it was blocked off, preventing people from coming or leaving.

After looking at every inch of square footage in this hallway, I found a small area for her and I to sit at. It was a small bench near the nurses' station, and it looked like it could fit three people on it so that's where I escorted her to. "Kim, what am I going to do without William?" And what about the girls? They're gonna be devastated when they find out that their father was murdered. And please don't let Mrs. Elaine die, who will raise them? I don't know anything about raising children. William did everything for those girls when they were with us."

"Let's just thank positive. Everything will work out." I told her. I mean, I didn't know what else to say.

"You know what? I hope that whoever was responsible for this get the death penalty." She roared. Telling her that everything would work out went over her head. Anger and rage began to fester inside her heart, and nothing would be more satisfying to her than to see the shooter pay dearly for killing William. I could only hope that my hitman isn't the suspect that they have in custody. And if they do, I can only pray that he keeps his mouth shut.

After sitting on the bench for what seemed like an eternity, the doctor that performed Mrs. Elaine approached us. Tammy and I gave him our undivided attention. "We've performed an intensive hour of surgery and was fortunatc to remove the bullet fragments from Mrs. Fisher's body. They'll be moving her into ICU where we will closely monitor her until she recovers." He explained.

"What are you gonna do about my husband?" Tammy blurted out.

"Ma'am I'm afraid there's nothing we can do for him." The doctor replied.

"I know you can't save him because he's already dead. I just need to know who's gonna take responsibility for the lack of security at this hospital? He was already here trying to recover from gunshot wounds from the first attempt on his life. So, for that same person to be able to get access to him again, is a clear sign that someone dropped the ball. And on top of that, he hasn't been moved. His body is still in that room lying-in blood-soaked sheets, riddled with bullets. It almost feels like no one cares." She expressed.

"There's nothing I can do about that. But I'm sure if you voice your concerns to one of these officers, they'll be able to help you. Now if you'll excuse me." The doctor said and then he walked off.

"I'll betcha' if I file a lawsuit against this hospital, you'll want to talk to me then," Tammy yelled out as the doctor headed in the opposite direction.

"Mrs. Slone you're gonna have to calm down. There are other patients on this floor." The officer who stood by us said.

"What's gonna happen if I don't?" She wanted to know.

Tammy wasn't feeling the doctor nor the police officers on this floor. At one point, I thought that she was going to fly off the handle and attack someone. Thankfully she didn't. I credit Sergeant Miles for it. Because while we were standing there, the elevator door chimed and then the doors slid open. Sergeant Miles stepped off the elevator first. Two uniformed police officers accompanied him. "Mrs. Weeks, will you come with me please?" He asked me, even though it didn't sound like a question. It was more of an order or demand in my eyes.

“Come with you where?” I asked him. The tone of his voice intimidated me.

“To the room where we were before, I left.” He told me as he stood before me.

"What is this about? Why are you taking her into a room?" Tammy interjected. She wanted to know what the cops wanted with me. I wanted to know too, but I played it cool like everything was going to be fine, even though I was having bad feelings on the inside of me.

Stuck My Foot in My Mouth

While I followed Sergeant Miles back to the room we were talking in before he excused himself, the two police officers with him followed. Immediately after we entered the room, Sergeant Miles instructed the two cops to stand outside the door until he told them otherwise. I was disturbed by Sergeant Miles' approach this time around, especially now that I know that they have a suspect in custody. All I could do now is hope and pray that it wasn't my hitman.

"Take a seat please." He started off.

I sat down and said, "What's on your mind?"

"I'm not sure if you know, but we have a suspect in custody." He said.

"No, I didn't know. But I'm glad you do. Throw the book at his ass! Especially after what he did to Mrs. Elaine. She didn't deserve what he did to her." I replied, knowing deep down in my heart that I would be devastated if it was my hitman. Not for the murder of William, but because Mrs. Elaine got caught up in the mix. She wasn't supposed to be hit. Point! Blank! Period!

"Mr. Slone didn't deserve what he got either." He corrected me.

"You're right, no, he didn't," I said nonchalantly. Because in my heart I wanted him dead. He was the reason why my best friend killed herself. She devoted her life to that selfish motherfucker. And all she got in return was divorce papers and $400 a month for child support.

“Ms. Weeks, is there something you want to say to me?”

“Not really. I mean, the doctor visited Tammy and I and told us that Mrs. Elaine is going to be fine, and I’m ecstatic about that.” I stated.

“Besides that,” he pressed me.

"What else do you want me to say?" I asked him. He was starting to get underneath my skin. But I knew what he was doing. Trying to get me to confess to something. But I wasn't going for the banana in the tailpipe.

“I want you to tell me why you set off the fire alarm before leaving this floor?” He asked me.

His question hit me like a ton of bricks. I mean, did he really just ask me about the fire alarm, that I ignited? How the fuck did he know this? It's not like this floor has a camera planted somewhere near the location of it. So, where is he getting his information from? I let out a long sigh and said, "Set off a fire alarm?! What do I look like a kid or something?"

“Mrs. Weeks I am trying to give you a life-line.” He pointed out.

“A lifeline for what? I didn’t set off the fire alarm.” I spat, trying to stand my ground. I knew it was important for me to project the body language of an innocent person, so I stuck my chest out and acted as if I was appalled by this accusation.

“Mrs. Weeks, we have you on camera. Now, tell me what your involvement is and then we’ll go from there.” He insisted.

Taken aback by his confession, all I could do was sit there in mere trepidation. What was I going to do now? What should I say? I mean, it’s not like what he’s saying isn’t true. He’s got me with my pants down.

“Are you going to answer my question?” He pressed me.

“What question?” I asked, even though I knew what his question was. In my mind, I needed those extra seconds to figure out whether or not I was going to tell him the truth. If I decide to tell him the truth, I’ll be putting myself in a box. A box that’ll probably be hard to get out of later down the road.

“Mrs. Weeks, tell me why you set off the fire alarm before you vacated the vicinity?”

"Sergeant Miles, I didn't set off the alarm, so if that's all you want to say to me, then I'm gonna head to the ICU so that I can check on Mrs. Elaine," I said and then I stood up and made two steps towards the door. On thc third step, Sergeant Miles stopped me in my tracks.

“I’m sorry Mrs. Weeks, but I’m afraid that I can’t let you go.” He said and then he grabbed me by my arm.

“You better get your damn hands off me.” I snapped, snatching my arm away from the detective. But as soon as I got him to release my arm, he grabbed it again. “What the fuck is wrong with you? Didn’t I tell you to get your hands off me?” I roared. It was as if he and I were playing dug-a-war with my arm.

"Mrs. Weeks, you are under arrest for willfully and maliciously tampering with fire alarm protection equipment system on the grounds of a state-funded medical facility." He started saying after he pulled handcuffs from a pocket near his gun and began to handcuff me.

“So, you’re arresting me?” I asked him, shocked that he was really going there with me.

"You leave me no choice, Mrs. Weeks. I've got you on tape." He told me as he tightened the cuffs around my wrists.

“Where are you taking me?” I wanted to know.

“I’m taking you to jail. From there, you’ll get processed and given a bond. I can’t say what will happen to you after that.” He replied sarcastically.

“This is unnecessary. You don’t have to take me out of here in handcuffs.” I stated. In reality, I knew that as soon as Tammy saw me like this, she would start asking a lot of questions. Questions that would have to be answered, whether today or tomorrow. Not only that, the mere embarrassment of being escorted out of the hospital was eating away at me too. Everyone will be looking at me and whispering. Am I gonna be able to handle that?

Sergeant Miles went radio silent until he opened the door where the two cops were standing and instructed them to take me down to the county jail. Shocked by the fact that I was on my way to jail, took me to another level of anxiety. What am I going to do now?

I hung my head low as soon as the cops grabbed me by the arms and lead me down the hall towards the elevator. And just like I imagined, every cop, nurse, and doctor standing around turned their attention towards me. Tammy was sitting down on the bench talking to someone on her cell phone when she saw me. I tried with everything in me to avoid eye contact with her, but she wasn't having it. I watched her through my peripheral vision as she stood up on her feet with a facial expression of horror. If I were a mind reader, I knew that she was wondering why I was in handcuffs. And when she stood there and spoke, I realized that I was right. "What are y'all doing? And why is she in handcuffs?" She spat while gritting her teeth.

“Please step back ma’am. This is police business.” One of the cops said.

“Police business my butt! Are you arresting her?” She wouldn’t let up.

“Yes, we are.” The same cop answered.

“For what?” Tammy’s questions continued.

"They're trying to say that I set off the fire alarm," I interjected. There was no way that I was going to let these cops belittle me. Not like this.

“No way. Are you serious?” She replied.

"Don't worry. After I settle this matter, I'll be back up here to check on Mrs. Elaine. So, keep your head up and I'll see you soon." I told her as the cops led me away.

Tammy stood in the middle of the hallway and watched as the police officers escorted me to the elevator. After the elevator door closed, I was out of eye's reach. Not to say that I was out of her mind because I knew that I wasn't. I'm sure being told that I was the one that set off the fire alarm has her questioning whether or not it's true. Hopefully, she doesn't believe it because if she does, then things will go downhill from here. I don't know her personally, but if she ever finds out that I had something to do with her husband's murder, she will do everything in her power to end me. My whole existence.

The ride from the hospital to the county jail didn't take long. Ten minutes exactly. Trying to get these lazy ass intake officers to process me was like pulling teeth. I sat in that freaking holding pod for three hours, if not more. Sitting in that small boxed room with five other women was a challenge. One of the women was a white girl and at least 22-years old. I sat there and watched her as she laid there, balled up in a fetal position against the wall, rocking back and forth and complained about how badly her body was aching. She was sweating profusely. The sight of her was becoming unbearable. "Why won't someone help her?" I asked, directing my question to the other four women. I was sitting amongst one white woman, two black women, and a Hispanic chick.

“You can’t help someone going through a heroin withdrawal.” A white woman noted.

“How do you know?” I wondered aloud.

“Trust me, I’ve been through enough of them to know the symptoms when I see ‘em.” She informed me.

“How long does she have to go through this?” I inquired.

“At least three more days.” She told me.

"Damn," I said and then I turned my attention to the intake officers walking around the jail processing area. The freedom they had to walk around and not be cramped up in close quarters I had to endure. I swear, it's so funny how something we take for granted turns into something so valuable. I know one thing, once I get out of here, I am never coming back. You can bet your last dollar on that.

"Whatcha' in here for?" A middle-aged, black woman asked me.

"They said they have me on camera tampering with a fire alarm," I said nonchalantly.

“That’s it?” The same black woman said.

“Yes, that’s it.”

“Well, at least you ain’t in here for a probation violation. I got three years over my head so I ain’t going home no time soon.” The other black woman interjected.

"I'm in here for beating a bitch ass!" The Latina woman blurted out. "I caught my husband coming out of his side bitch's house again, so I had to make my presence be known."

"So, did you win the fight?" The white chick asked.

"Yep, I sure did." The Latina woman bragged as she swayed her head back and forth, giving off the Cardi B' persona. Cardi B' looked better, though.

The Latina chick continued to brag about how she pulled the side chick's hair and kicked her while she was down on the ground. The whole story sounded like bull shit ass girl's going wild video. If I didn't have all this mess on my mind, I probably would've joined in and laughed with the other ladies listening to the Hispanic chick describe every detail of the fight. She went on and on until the intake officer opened the door and called my name. "Weeks," The white officer said aloud.

I stood up on my feet. "Yes," I replied.

"Come with me." She said.

Without saying another word, I walked towards the intake officer and as soon as I approached her, she pushed the door open enough so I could walk across the threshold. "Follow me over to that counter area." She instructed me after she pushed the holding cell door close.

It didn't take long for the intake officer to process me in their system. After she took my photo, finger-printed me and entered my personal information in their criminal database, she escorted me to another room to see the magistrate. To my surprise, I was told to stand in front of a TV monitor, and after I had done so, the monitor powered on and then a white, fat ole' man appeared, dressed in a cotton button-up shirt and a cheap-looking tie.

He looked at me and then he looked down at a file on his deck. "Can you tell me your name?" He started off.

"Kim Weeks."

"Date of birth?"

"July 17, 1977."

"Where do you work?"

"I'm a real estate investor?" I lied. Well, technically I could be considered an investor. My ex-husband and I both owned the night club he still runs today.

"What's your current address?"

"It's 4012 Park Chester Drive, Virginia Beach, Virginia, 23410."

"How long have you been at that residence?"

"A little over a year now."

"Okay, let's see here," he said and then he paused, "You've been charged with one count of unlawfully, tampering with, or otherwise interfering with the operation of a fire safety devise and inciting harm to human life, which is a Class C felony and if convicted, you could serve up to one year in prison and pay a fine not exceeding five thousand dollars.” He added and then he looked back at me. “Do you understand the charges?” He wanted to know.

"Yes, sir," I replied.

“Great, so I’m gonna set your bail at $2,500. Now if you bail out, all you would need is 10%.” He explained.

"Thank you," I told him.

“You’re welcome.” He said and then the monitor went dark.

“Could I get my phone call now?” I asked the intake officer.

“Yes, you may.” She said and we both exited that room.

Let the Games Begin

It shocked Julian when I called him and told him where I was. "Just hold on and I'll be there within the hour." He assured me. And what do you know, he showed up within an hour. It felt good to hear my name called by one of the intake officers. It felt even better when I walked out of the front door of the county jail. The breath of fresh air was undoubtfully the best feeling in the world. "Are you ready to tell me what happened?" He didn't waste time asking me.

"It's a long story," I replied.

"I'm all ears." He said.

"My deceased best friend committed suicide and shortly thereafter her ex-husband was shot in his home a few days ago. He survived the shooting and was taken to the hospital. Now don't quote me on this, but it's rumored that the person that shot him found out that he was still alive and came back to finish the job. But what's really upsetting was that my best friend's mother was in the room visiting him when the shooting happened. Thank God. she didn't die. But she is in ICU."

“So, when do you come in the picture?” He pressed the issue.

“Well, they’re saying that right after the fire alarm sounded off, that’s when the shooting occurred.”

“Is that what happened?” He asked, looking at me strangely.

“Of course not.” I spat. “And I’m appalled that you would ask me that question.”

"Come on now Kim, I'm like an officer of the courts, so I've gotta ask questions like that; especially if I'm involved with someone that has a brush with the law." He explained.

“Look, I understand all of that. But that’s not me. I don’t do things like that. I’ve got a lot to lose.” I lied, trying to keep a straight face.

He cracked a smile and said, “Now see, that’s what I like to hear.”

I smiled back and then I shifted my attention to the and cars and people we rode by. It seemed like everyone I saw didn't have a care in the world. They looked stress-free. But I knew that underneath their facial expressions had something buried deep inside of their hearts. Look at me for instance, on the surface, it looks like I'm happy and got the entire world in the palm of my hands, but I'm hurt, scorned and bitter. My ex-husband stole my heart and when he was done with it, he tossed it in the nearest trash can. I walked away from my marriage with nothing. No kids, no life; nothing. I never thought in a million years that my life would be like this. I guess all I can do now is pick up the pieces and move forward. Find a place where I can be happy. Who knows, maybe this guy Julian could help me do it. Only time will tell.

I talked Julian into dropping me back off at the hospital so I could get my car. But before I exited his car, he made me promise that I wasn't going back into the hospital. "Don't give those cops another reason to lock you up." He said.

"I won't," I assured him and then I got into my car. I even started up the ignition and drove around the parking lot like I was leaving. But as soon as he drove away, I did a 180-degree turn and headed to the opposite side of the hospital and found a nice parking space between two big trucks.

Immediately after I powered off the ignition, I sat in my car for a few minutes, trying to figure out how I was going to approach the situation if I ran into Tammy or one of the detectives working on that floor. I knew trying to avoid contact with the cops would be my best course of action, but will it be that easy?

After sitting in my car for a total of five minutes, I got out and walked inside the hospital. From the looks of things, the hospital seemed like it had calmed down. On the first floor, I only saw one cop. I ducked him and walked in the other direction just in case my photo was circulating around here somewhere.

Instead of taking the elevator I walked the five flights of stairs; taking my time and walking very carefully so that no one heard me. For some reason, I wasn't that afraid to enter back on the fifth floor. I guess it was because I had already had my run-in with the cops and getting arrested because of it.

Once I had approached the exit door of that floor, I took a deep breath, exhaled and said, "Kim you got it. Don't let these people put fear in you. The worst part is over." Two seconds after giving myself words of encouragement, I grab the exit door handle and then I pulled it open slowly. I've got to admit, that my heartbeat sped up a little bit, but it was nothing to be concerned with. It was just a feeling of not knowing what was around the corner.

This time around, it was quiet. There weren't a whole bunch of different voices talking at the same time. I did hear two people conversing, but it was nothing like earlier. This made me comfortable, to say the least, and that's when I entered on the floor.

When I zoomed in on the two voices that I heard from the stairwell, I realize that it was a doctor and a nurse talking about a patient. I didn't recognize these two people, so I walked by them with my head hung low and prayed that they did recognize me.

“Has someone contacted her next of kin?” I heard the doctor ask the nurse.

“Yes, we’ve contacted her sister and her niece, but they both live in Delaware.”

“Any word on when they’ll be here to sign off some documents?”

"They said that they could be here in a couple of hours." The nurse responded. Listening to the nurse and doctor gave me an eerie feeling that they were talking about Mrs. Elaine. I mean, who else could it be? Mrs. Elaine has relatives in the state of Delaware and North Carolina. So what are the odds that another patient here needs relatives to come to the hospital and sign off on medical waivers?

Feelings of anxiety and desperation wanted me to turn around and ask them if they were talking about Mrs. Elaine, but I knew that that wouldn't be a good idea. I needed to keep a low profile while I am here. Being escorted out of the hospital in handcuffs embarrassed the hell out of me. So, I refuse to allow that to happen again.

A couple of hours earlier, I remember the doctor that performed the emergency surgery on Mrs. Elaine said that she was transferred to ICU, so I followed the hospital map on the wall and it took me straight there.

When I approached the double doors for the unit, I hit the button on the right side of the wall to open both doors. Only a couple of seconds later, did the doors open and when it did I walked inside. This was a totally different department of thc hospital, so I felt comfortable being here. Seeing the different faces of these nurses and doctors allowed me to be myself and not be so uptight. I can only hope that no one from the other floor comes anywhere near here. If they do, the drama will follow.

I walked up to the nurses' station and found two nurses sitting behind the desk. Both women were Caucasian. But I could tell that one woman was older than the other one. I spoke to them both and then I asked them for Mrs. Ellen Fisher's room number. "Are you a relative?" The older nurse spoke first.

"Yes, I'm her niece." I lied.

"Can I see your ID?" she insisted.

"Wait a minute," I stated calmly. "I'm gotta show you my ID to see a family member?" I added.

"Yes ma'am, you do." The same nurse said.

"We don't have the same last name," I told her.

"That's fine, we only need it to put it on her visitor login sheet." The other nurse interjected.

I sifted through my handbag, grabbed my driver's license and handed it to the older nurse. "Here you go," I said.

She took it, looked at it and then she wrote my name down on a patient's visitor sheet. "You can have this back." She replied. "She's in room 517," she added.

When I took my driver's license back, I thanked her and then I headed to Mrs. Elaine's room.

I didn't know what to expect after I walk into her room. Will she have an oxygen mask on her face? Bandages all over her body? Will she be awake? And if so, will she know who I am? I swear, having all of these thoughts running through my head at once was finally taken a toll on me. I guess I can only wish for the best but expect the worst.

The door to Mrs. Elaine's room was slightly ajar so I pushed it open and walked into the room. I saw her feet covered with the white bed sheet and after walking further into the room I found that same sheet covering most of her body. Her arms had multiple IV needles inserted into her skin to keep track of her vitals, keep her hydrated with IV fluids, and they were even given her a blood transfusion. I'm assuming they were doing this because she lost a lot of blood after being shot multiple times. Seeing her like this, broke my heart. She's not supposed to be in here fighting for her life. She supposed to be at home spending time with her grandchildren. Damn! I wish I could turn the clock back.

"What are you doing here?" I heard a voice behind me say.

Startled by the sudden notion of a visitor, I whirled my head around and saw Tammy standing in the hallway behind me. Her eyes were bloodshot red. She looked like she had been crying for days. But what stuck out more with me was the tone of her voice. This wasn't the Tammy I left in the hospital a couple of hours ago. This was the nasty Tammy that called the cops on Mariah and me when we were on their front porch. The one that lied and got the restraining order on us. Yeah, that one. So, I knew shit was about to hit the fan.

"Wait, did I miss something?" I asked her, trying hard to bite my tongue. Right now, wasn't the time for her and I to have a squabble, especially in or outside of Mrs. Elaine's room.

Before she could respond to my question another chick walked up and stood next to Tammy. She looked like she and Tammy could be sisters; Tammy being the other sister and all. The resemblance was crazy. "Is everything all right." The chick asked after taking a sip from her soda bottle.

"Oh, everything is fine." I rushed to answer the sister's question.

"It won't be if you don't leave." She warned me.

"Leave from where?" I asked sarcastically.

"So, no one told you?"

"Told me what?"

"That you're band from this hospital. I saw the tape. You set off the fucking alarm and as soon as they link you and the killer that murdered my husband, you're going to prison and will never see the light of day again." She continued as she gritted her teeth.

"Bitch, you are delusional if you think I had something to do with your husband's murder. You need to do some investigating and find out the names of loan sharks he owes. He's in a lot of debt sweetie!" I hissed. Boy, I could tell that I had struck a nerve. But quiet as kept, William didn't owe money to any loan sharks. I only said that so she could get off my back. I wanted her to feel the hurt and anxiety I was feeling.

"You are a liar! My husband doesn't owe anyone shit! Take that back. You're trying to tarnish his name and I won't have it." She ranted. But instead of fueling that fire she and I ignited I turned around and walked over to Mrs. Elaine's bed. I told her how much I loved her, and I apologized to her for what happened to her. I even kissed her on her forehead and told her that I would be back to see her soon.

While I was exciting her room, Tammy had rallied up a couple of nurses to remove me from the hospital. "She's the one that set off the fire alarm. The homicide detectives escorted her out of here a few hours ago and now she's back." She was screaming and yelling. "I'm calling the officers now." She threatened all while keying in the numbers to one of the detectives' cellular phone. One of the nurses walked up to me and asked me nicely if I would leave the premises. I assured her that I was leaving so she thanked me and then she stood there and watched me walk away. Once again, I felt a sense of embarrass-ment. I wasn't escorted out of the hospital in handcuffs, but I was told to leave while Tammy made a scene. I don't know which incident was worse. I guess it's a tossup.

Making the Call

The walk back to my car seemed long for some reason. It felt like I was walking in slow motion; like this wasn't my reality. I do know one thing; Tammy is on to me and I need to figure out my next course of action.

After mulling over a list of things that I needed to do, calling my hitman was at the top of my list. The cops mentioned earlier that they had a suspect in custody, so calling him from my cellphone wouldn't be the smartest thing to do. I needed one of those burner phones and I knew one place that sold them. My ex-husband used to keep a slew of those pre-paid cellphones. He used them to call his bitches on. He even used them to communicate with his bootleg liquor connection. They worked wonders for him, so I knew I was going to be fine.

The name of the corner store that sold those instant pre-paid phones was called Quick Shop. Hoodlums and drug addicts hung out around this place. When I pulled up and saw how crowded it was, I almost attempted to leave. Getting robbed in a hood like this would be a person like me's worse nightmare. But then I remembered that I grew up in the hood, so just be normal. Act like you're in your element and everything would be cool. And guess what? It worked. I got out of my car, spoke to the guys that spoke to me, went inside the store, purchased one of those burner phones and then I got back in my car and left. It was that simple. Now just imagine life being just like that.

I drove away from the corner store and headed back towards my apartment. I didn't go all the way home though. I was anxious to get the cellphone activated so I pulled over and parked my car in the parking lot of a Walmart that was a few miles away from where I lived.

After I powered on the phone, I followed every instruction laid out on the product page and to my surprise, I activated the cell phone in a matter of two minutes. Now it was time to call my hitman. "Please pick up," I said in a whisper waiting for the phone to ring. DINGGGG! DINGGG! Hearing the sound of this guy's cell phone ringing and waiting for him or someone to pick up was becoming agonizing. My stomach started creating little small knots and they were jumping around like crazy. Taking on all of these mental and physical emotions took me to another level of anxiety. Fear had officially taken over my body and I have lost total control. This had to stop.

I sat in my car and listened to the phone ring at least eight times and my hitman didn't answer. Actually, no one answered for that matter. Was this a good sign or a bad one?

"Come on dude, answer your phone," I said, crossing my fingers and hoping that he'd answer. Well, at this point, I would take anyone. I just need to know what's going on.

Again, I sat in my car and listened to the phone ring back to back. This time it rang seven times and then the line went radio silent. I took the phone away from my ear and slammed it down on the passenger side floor of my car. "Fuck! Fuck! Fuck! Answer your gotdamn phone will you!" I snapped while punching the steering wheel of my car.

Furious by not knowing what was going on was talking a toll on me. And if I don't find out what's happening soon, then who knows what's going to happen to me.

I stopped trying to call the hitman after the third try. I figured what's the use? He wasn't going to answer it anyway. So, put my time and energy elsewhere, I climbed on my living room sofa and powered on the TV. And then there it was, one of the news networks was being filmed standing outside of the hospital covering the events that happened today. I sat up straight and turned up the volume so I could hear every word.

“I was told by law enforcement that they have Adam Blue in custody. He is believed to have killed William Slone and wounded Mrs. Elaine Fisher while dressed in hospital scrubs. I was also told that Mrs. Fisher is in an Intensive Care Unit and is expected to fully recover. No word on whether or not the suspect that you see in this photo committed this heinous crime alone or if he had an accomplice. So, if you have any information that would help homicide detectives solve this devastating crime, please call 1-800-Lockuup. Back to you Melissa." The reporter said and then the camera shifted to another reporter.

Oh my God. It was true, the cops had my hitman and had his picture plastered all over the fucking TV for the world to see. What was I going to do now? The cops got his dummy in jail. Now how did that happen? He was supposed to be a professional hitman and he came highly recommended. So, how did he allow the cops to catch him? Damn! I should've listened to my intuition and went elsewhere after he botched the job with William the first time around. He's nothing but an amateur getting paid high bounties for jobs that I probably could've done myself. In the meantime, I've gotta' find out what's gonna happen next? Will they give him a bail? Or keep him locked up? On top of that, I have no one to talk to. I know I have Julian, but I can't tell him I've been putting bounties on bitches' heads and paying my hitman to take them out. He would look at me like I was a fucking mad woman. He may even report me to the fucking cops. I swore that I wasn't going back to jail, and I mean it.

From getting locked up behind the fire alarm bullshit to the feud Tammy and I got into earlier, my head has been spinning nonstop. I swear I don't know if I'm coming or going. I've been on edge all night and I need something to relax me. Having some company would do me just fine and I can't think of no one else but Julian, so I grabbed my cell phone from the nightstand next to my bed and dialed his number. Thankfully he answered it on the second ring. “What’s up?” I asked him.

"Nothing much. In my office doing paperwork on a guy that skipped court this morning." He replied. I heard him typing on his computer keyboard, so I knew he was working. "What's up with you gorgeous?" He asked me.

I wanted to tell him that I was in a fucked up situation and that if I had the slightest idea of how I was going to get out of it. I even wanted to tell him that the shit I’ve gotten myself in could potentially land me in prison for the rest of my life. I wondered how he’d take it. Would he leave me? Or would he help me sort this thing out? Time will tell. “I’m chilling. Just lying around watching TV and thinking about you.” I finally said.

“Oh really?!” He replied in a bubbly manner. He was excited to hear me say that I was thinking about him.

“Yes, really/” I replied. I wanted to sound like I was into him and was beginning to like the idea of bringing him into my world. In reality, I did like him, but not the way I was leading on. Unbelievably, I was still in love with my ex-husband. I can’t tell you why. I guess, one day I will be able to answer that question. So, for right now, I’m gonna focus on Julian and see where this goes.

“Whatcha’ doing later?”

“Nothing. Why? Are you stopping by?”

“I can.”

“Well, make it happen.”

“Want me to pick up something to eat?”

“Let’s order a pizza after you get here.”

“Okay, let’s do that.” He decided.

“Do you know what time I should expect you?”

“Give me until 8 o’clock.”

“Perfect. So, I guess I’ll see you then.”

“Roger that.” He agreed and then we said goodbye.

I tried to relax and take the load off while I waited for Julian to come over but I couldn't seem to stay in one place. In five minutes, I got up from the sofa, walked to the kitchen, from the kitchen to the bathroom, from the bathroom and back to the kitchen. I even peered out the window a few times as well. I believe I saw one or two undercover police vehicles parked outside of my place. I swear, it spooked the hell out of me too. It's like they won't leave me alone. Vowing to stay away from the windows, I sat down on my living room sofa and tried to watch a movie, but I couldn't get into it. Every time I start watching a scene, my mind would drift off and think about my last run-in with Tammy. The fact that she jumped ship and now believes that I had something to do with William's death and Mrs. Elaine's near-death experience, makes me angry. Not only that, I don't know the hitman on a personal level so I'm not sure what he's capable of doing. What I need to do is reach out to my private investigator. He's the one that introduced me to him, so maybe he'd be able to shed some light on who and what I was doing with.

"Here goes nothing," I said underneath my breath after I grabbed my cell phone from the coffee table in from of me. My heart rate picked up speed after I dialed the number and listened to it ring. I tried to rehearse what to say if he answered my call, but my words started jumbling up in my head. The only thing that was clear in my mind was that I needed to distance myself from this situation and do it fast. Hopefully the private investigator could help me figure that out.

"This is Private Investigator Tillman. How can I help you?" He said.

"Hi Mr. Tillman, this is Kim Weeks, how are you?" I replied calmly. I wanted to project a sense of composure even though I was a basket case. If he was standing in front of me right now, I'd probably jump into his arms and ask him to save me from all this shit that was about to hit the fan. Then I would smack the shit out of him and ask him why he set me up with that bootleg ass bounty hunter. He was supposed to get rid of all the shit that plagued my life, but what he has done was fucked it up. I'm worse off than where I started.

"Oh hi, Ms. Weeks. What can I help you with?"

"I have a big problem. And I don't know how to get out of it."

"I'm sorry to hear that. What's going on?"

"The guy you referred me to isn't working out."

"What guy are you talking about?" He asked. But he said it nonchalantly. Like he's trying to choose his words correctly.

"The guy. You know." I tried to jog his memory.

"Who am I talking to again?" He asked me.

Now, this motherfucker is throwing in the who am I talking to question in the mix. This bastard knew who he was speaking to. "Mr. Tillman, this is Kim Weeks. You helped me with my divorce case with my ex-husband."

"Are you sure you got the right number?" He questioned me.

"Mr. Tillman, what fucking games are you playing. This is Kim Weeks. You introduced me to that fucking maniac and now I'm in a load of shit because of him." I shouted through the phone line.

"I'm sorry ma'am but I'm afraid that you have the wrong number." He replied and then the phone line went radio silent.

Devastated by his dismissive behavior, I slammed my cell phone down on the sofa. "Motherfucka!" I roared and jumped up to my feet.

He knew who the fuck I was! Trying to pretend like he didn't. I know he saw the hitman on TV. That's why he didn't want to talk about it over the phone. But it's alright. This won't be the last time he hears from me.

Keeping Secrets

Julian finally stopped by. But when he got here, I kind of gave him the cold shoulder. I didn't mean to do it, but after that encounter, I had with Mr. Tillman, I couldn't get into a good mood.

We went into the living room and sat down on the sofa after we grabbed pizza slices from the pizza box in the kitchen. I played around with my slice while Julian scoffed his two slices down in a matter of four minutes, or maybe less. "I take it that you're not hungry." He commented while he worked on his last slice.

I sighed. "I just got a lot on my mind," I told him.

“I know you do. But don’t sweat it, you’ll be alright.” He said, trying to console me.

But it didn't work. There's nothing he could say right now that would console me. I was knee-deep in shit and I can't tell you how things will end for me. I do know that I will find the answer sooner than later.

“If you say so,” I replied.

“Before I left the office today, I got my assistant Charmaine to look into that situation you’re in….” He started off saying but I cut him off.

“Why would you get her to do that? I don’t want her in my business.” I spat. I mean, why would he do that? I don’t know her.

“Calm down. She works for me. And besides, she’s the one that processed your paperwork so I could bail you out of jail.” He replied after stuffing the last piece of pizza into his mouth.

I sucked my teeth. “What did she find out?” I asked him even though I was afraid to hear his answer. For all I know, she could’ve found out how deep I was in that hospital incident.

"She didn't find out anything. The only that popped up under your name was the arrest warrant for the fire alarm situation."

“That’s it?” I wondered aloud.

"Yeah," He answered. And then he said, "Is there supposed to be something else?"

“No,” I replied in a *why would you ask me something like that* manner.

“Well, don’t kill me for asking.” He joked.

"Shut up!" I said, giving him a half-smile and then I smacked his arm.

“Now see, that’s what I wanna see. A big ole’ pretty smile.” He smiled at me.

"But I don't wanna smile," I said and nudged him.

“Why not?” He pressed the issue.

“Because of everything that’s going on. Do you know how embarrassing it was to get escorted out of the hospital in handcuffs? I’ve never had anything like that to happen to me.” I told him, without telling him everything that’s been weighing heavily on me. If only I could pour my heart out to him. But since I can't, I will continue to carry this load alone.

I finally got into the movie Julian and I was watching. But the ambiance that he and I finally created was short-lived by a phone call. I looked at the time on the clock in my living room and it clearly stated that it was 10:05 pm. I pretended to be engrossed in the movie while he answered the call. "A.J. Bondsman," he said.

I couldn't hear the caller, but Julian made it easy to decipher what that caller was saying by what he was saying. "What's the bond?" I heard him say and then he fell silent. "Will you be the one signing the bail?" He added. "Okay, well bring me $2,500 and meet me outside the jail in thirty minutes." He continued and then he ended the call.

"I know what that means," I commented.

"Don't worry, I will be back. Well, that is, if you want me to." He said.

"Of course, I do. Call me when you're done." I insisted.

"I will." He promised and then he kissed me on the forehead. I walked him to the front door and watched him walk away after he exited my place. This moment was bittersweet. My heart wanted him to stay here and comfort me with everything going on in my life. But the other side of me wanted him to give me some space to figure things out. If I don't, then I'd surely create my demise.

Making the Trip

Julian never came back to my place last night. He called me and told me that things had really busy for him. So, I told him I understood and in turn, he promised to take me out to lunch today. I thought the gesture was nice and told him that I'd stop by his office so that we could go to lunch together instead of separate cars. Once we agreed to the time, we shared a few more pleasantries and then we ended the call.

Now my main reason for leaving my place today was to make a special visit to Mr. Tillman's office. The fact that he denied knowing me last night when I asked his ass on the phone was an insult, especially with all the money I gave his ass to investigate my ex-husband and his fucking mistresses. He was gonna hear my mouth today.

Mr. Tillman's office was about ten miles away from my place, so it didn't take me long to get there. Immediately after I parked my car, I stormed in the office building. His office was on the first floor of a two-floor building. I had to walk down a long hallway and pass a utility closet, and the ladies' restroom to get to Mr. Tillman's office.

I was greeted by his receptionist. Her name was Claire and she was a broke down version of the pop singer Britney Spears. I'm talking about cheap looking extensions, knock-off clothes and the whole bit. She was a complete mess and it wouldn't surprise me if she was fucking her boss, Mr. Tillman. "Can I help you?" she asked me, trying to look like an authoritative person. Even her speech was off course. On several occasions, I wondered why she even worked for him. He was a black ex. cop, with a shaky career on the police force. But then it hit me, he hired her because he's fucking her and on top of that, he's using her white face to represent his business. What a win-win for him, but not so much for her. "I'm here to see Mr. Tillman," I replied, giving her an angelic smile. I didn’t want to give her the impression that I was upset about something, more importantly, that her boss was the cause of it.

“Oh hi, I remember you.” She acknowledged.

"Yes, it's been a couple of months now," I commented.

“Do you have an appointment?” She wanted to know and then she shifted her focus to the small calendar on her desk. I noticed her sifting through the list to see if I was on it.

“No, I don’t. But he knew I was stopping in for a second.” I lied.

"Well, I think he's on a call. But let me see." She said and then she picked up her phone and called him. "Mr. Tillman, I have a visitor." She spoke into the phone. "What's your name again?" she turned her focus back towards me.

“Kim. Kim Weeks,” I said reluctantly because I knew he was going to throw some shit in the mix. You know like, tell her that he’s busy and for me to make an appointment. But I wasn't gonna let him play that game with me. Nope! Not today!

"It's Mrs. Weeks," she repeated what I said. Not even a second later, she looked back at me and said, "He said this is not a good time for him and that if you make an appointment with me, he'll be available to talk to you then,"

“See, I fucking knew it.” I spat. “I knew he was gonna try to throw me a curb ball. But not today, especially with all the money I gave him. Oh no, he will talk to me now!” I shouted and then I stormed down a nearby hallway, reaching his office door four seconds later. Without knocking on the door, I turned the knob and forced it open. Our eyes connected instantly. I could tell that he was trying to make it to his door before I got there, but I didn't give him enough time to do so. “So, whatcha' trying to do? Lock the door on me?” I roared.

“No, no, no.....” he began to say but I cut him off.

“No, no, my ass!” I replied as I stood in the middle of the office floor. “I called you yesterday and you acted like you didn't know who I was. What was that all about?” I shouted louder.

“I'm sorry but I had to. I saw the news.” He tried to explain.

“Well, you should've said that.” I hissed at him. My blood was boiling at this point.

“You can't say something like that over the phone.”

“Look, fuck all of that, what’s up with that guy? Think he might rat me out?”

"I'm not sure. I don't know him all that well. I was introduced to him through a mutual friend not long after you retained me to investigate your ex-husband."

"Wait, so you're saying that you didn't know that guy?" I asked. By now I was about to jump out of my skin.

“No. I reached out to an old buddy and asked him if he knew somebody that could do the jobs for you and he called me back the next day with that guy’s number.”

"But, you told me that he came highly recommended." I snapped. Because now this fool was fucking with my intelligence.

“Yes, I know. And I told you that because that’s what I was told when the number was given to me.” He spoke apologetically.

“Aghhhhhh!” I shouted. “Do you know what you did by introducing me to that fucking psychopath?”

“Shhhhhhhh…” he said and then he rushed over and closed the door to his office. Besides myself and Mr. Tillman, no one else was in the office, so this was a clear indication that he didn’t want his secretary to hear our conversation. “I am so sorry that I didn’t vet him first.”

“Fuck that! It’s too late for apologies. I need to figure a way out of this shit! For all I know that motherfucker could’ve implicated me.”

“I don’t think that he’s that type of guy.” Mr. Tillman tried to pacify me. But I wasn’t going for that *banana in the tailpipe* shenanigan.

“I’m sorry but I can’t afford to take your word on that. Look where that has gotten me.” I replied sarcastically as I sat down on a chair near his desk.

He took a seat back in the chair behind his desk. “Has he tried to contact you?” Mr. Tillman asked me.

“No, he hasn’t.”

"Well, that's a good sign." He said, trying to lighten the mood between him and me.

"Look forget all of that, my main focus right now is to figure out my next step. As I'm sure you know, I got arrested two days ago for setting off the fire alarm at the hospital……" I started but Mr. Tillman interjected by saying, "No wait, you were arrested two days ago?"

“Yes. I thought you knew about it.”

"No, I didn't," he replied as if he was trying to digest what I had just admitted to doing.

“What made you set off the fire alarm?” He asked, giving me a puzzled facial expression.

I hesitated for a second because I didn’t want to give him details of my role in the murder of my best friend’s ex-husband. But then I realized that I had already let the cat out the bag so why hold back now. I mean, he was the one that introduced the hitman and I so he’s as much as an accomplice as I am.

"Look, I contracted him to knock off my best friend's ex-husband, but when he went to execute the job, he missed the vital organs and the motherfucker survived the attack. So, to be able to finish the job, he had to go to the hospital to do it. But that meant that he was going to need a distraction. So, that's where I came in. He needed me to sound off the fire alarm to divert the attention of the hospital staff and that's what I did." I explained.

"And you got arrested for that?" He pressed the issue.

"Yes," I said and then I paused to take a deep breath, "and when I was confronted by the cops, they said that they had me on camera committing the act."

"So, as for right now, they haven't connected you to the murder of your best friend's ex-husband?"

"No, they haven't. That's why I called you yesterday to find out what type of guy the hitman was. If he'd snitch on me? Or if he's one of those dudes that live by the street code."

"I see your concern." He said and then he looked down at his wristwatch. "Well, I guess I'm gonna have to cut this short. My next appointment is in five minutes." He added. And this did not bode well with me. I got upset with him all over again with his dismissive ass demeanor. If you aren't giving this fool a check then he has no desire to talk to you.

"There you go with that *I gotta another appointment* bullshit!" I hissed as I rolled my eyes at him.

"No, it's true. I do have an appointment in five minutes." He tried assuring me, pulling out his cell phone and showing the date and times of appointments that he has on his calendar from the screen.

I stood up from the chair because quite frankly, I had had enough of his ass. But after I got up, I leaned over towards him and said, "Everything that I said to you today better not leave this room and if it does, then you're going down with me. Do you understand me?"

"Yes, I understand. Our conversation will remain confidential." He tried to assure me.

"You better hope so because I will not take that fall alone. Not only that, I will let the world know that you're a pedophile and that you like watching kid porn."

"No, that's not true!" he shot up to his feet. "Why would you say something like that?"

"Because I can. Now fuck with my freedom and see what happens." I warned him. "Oh yeah, and when I call you or stop by here to talk to you, you better welcome me with open arms or there's gonna be consequences to that as well," I added and then I exited his office.

On my way out, I walked back by his dumb ass secretary. She told me to have a nice day, and in exchange, I told her to fuck off. She didn't see that coming. But I did.

Lunch Time

Still worked up by the mishap at Mr. Tillman's office, I took a breath and exhaled as soon as I stepped outside in the cool air. It was 70 degrees outside, and it felt good. The breeze alone was breathtaking and as I took each step to my car, I felt reinvigorated for some reason. But I couldn't figure out why. Was it because I went off on Mr. Tillman? Or was it the fact that I've gotten one step closer to finding out what kind of person the hitman was? Whatever it is, I'm gonna ride that train until I'm tossed off it.

In route to Julian's office, my cell phone rings, and I instantly smile because the call was coming from him. "What's up?" I said cheerfully.

"Where are you?" He wanted to know.

"On my way to your office. Remember we're supposed to have lunch?"

"How could I forget that?"

"You better not."

"Well, I only called to tell you that I would be running about 15 minutes late. So, let Charmaine know who you are and wait in the lounge area."

"Okay. Will do." I promised.

From there he made a few flirtatious comments about how he can't wait to smell my neck and rub on my beautiful feet. I mean, he really knew how to make me feel good about myself. He sure made up for all the bullshit my ex-husband didn't do.

Julian was definitely a step above the rest. Let's see how long he stays like this.

We ended our call after I told him that I had just pulled up to his office. "Don't forget to tell Charmaine who you are. She knows that you're coming."

"I will," I assured.

Julian's bail-bondsman office was a storefront property in the hood area of downtown. He was right in the heart of Kerry Park, one of the roughest urban communities in Tidewater. Julian knew what he was doing when he put his office here. I'm sure the majority of his clients are drug dealers. So, why not have your office where the drugs are being sold because now their buddies won't have to travel far to get Julian to bail them out of jail.

I made sure I locked my car doors after getting out of the car. I activated my car alarm too and then I headed towards the building. Unfortunately, when I approached the front door it was locked, plus there was a *be back in 10 minutes* sign hanging up on the other side of the glass door. "Be back in 10 minutes, huh? Your ass is supposed to be here now." I commented, mocking the sign.

"I am allowed to take two ten-minute breaks a day." I heard a voice behind me say. Surprised by the unexpected voice coming from behind me, I turned around and there standing before me was a young, beautiful, caramel-colored full-figure woman that resembled Jennifer Hudson before her Weight Watcher days. Her hair was thick and healthy-looking. She even dressed nice. I couldn't say anything bad about her.

“Sorry about that. I’m a little impatient at times.” I confessed and then I extended my hand. “My name is Kim. Julian told me that you’d be expecting me.” I changed the subject.

She shook my hand. “I know who you are. Julian has a photo of you in your file.” She said.

I chuckled bashfully. "Oh yeah, you're right," I commented.

“Come on, let’s go inside.” She instructed me after unlocking the glass front door. She walked across the threshold first and then I followed her. The moment after we entered the office, she took the sign down from the glass door and then she scrolled over to her desk and tucked her handbag in a drawer behind her desk. “You can sit wherever you like.” She insisted.

Once I sat down on the lounge chair, I sat up straight and then I placed my handbag on my lap like the prim and proper woman that I was. I saw her watching my every move after I held my head high.

“Can I get you a cup of coffee?” She asked.

“No, I’m good but thank you!” I replied.

“So, where are you guys going to lunch?” She questioned me.

"I think we agreed on going to the sushi restaurant in Town Center," I told her.

She chuckled. “Now that’s a first.”

“What do you mean?” I inquired.

“I didn’t know he liked sushi. This must’ve been your idea.” She commented.

"It was," I said confidently.

“So, how is everything going with your charge?” She changed the subject.

“What do you mean?” I asked her, trying to get clarity about why she’s so concerned about the status of my crime.

“Have you retained an attorney yet?”

“No, not yet.”

"Why not? Your charge is a very serious crime." She advised me. But I saw right through her façade. I wanted to tell her to mind her fucking business, but then that wouldn't have been a nice thing to say; especially to a young, dumbass ho that works for a guy I like very much.

"Don't worry, I've got everything under control," I replied sarcastically, giving her the biggest smile that I could muster up. I wanted to send the message, that you're a little girl in a grown woman's world, so stay in your lane.

“I’m sure you do.” She replied casually and then she gave me the same smirked that I gave her.

“So, how long have you worked for Julian?” I shifted the conversation.

“For about two years now.” She said boastfully.

“Are you his only employee?”

“The one and only. Now there was another bondsman working here and he had two employees, but it didn’t work out, so they parted way.”

“How long ago was that?”

“About a year ago.” She answered and then she shifted the direction of the conversation again. “So, how did you two meet?”

“Believe me, it’s a long story.” I lied. Truth is, I wasn’t in the mood to talk to this young girl about how I met her boss. This was not a Cinderella story. Bitch! Get a life, will you?!

"Well, he and I met on a dating website over two years ago. We dated for a bit. Then we broke up because he said that I was too immature for him. A few months passed and I happen to see him at the mall. We stood there and talked for a couple of minutes. You know, catching up and things. And somehow it came up that he needed an office assistant. And at that time, I had needed a job too. So, he hired me, and the rest is history."

"Sounds like a story out of a fairy tale book," I commented nonchalantly because I couldn't care less about how they met. What I am concerned about is the fact that he fucked her, which makes me wonder if they’ve had sex since she’s been working for him? If that’s the case, then I need to distance myself ASAP.

“That’s what everyone says when I tell ‘em. So, are you married?”

"If I were, I wouldn't be here now," I rcplied in a matter of fact kind of way.

"Well, have you ever been married?" She pressed me.

"Yes, I have. Seven years."

"Why did y'all get divorced?"

"He cheated."

"Come on now, married men always cheat." She stated.

"Not all men." I disagreed.

"Did y'all have any kids?"

"You sure ask a lot of questions," I commented and then I laughed it off.

"Don't mind me, I do this to everybody." She replied. And before she could utter another word, the office telephone began to ring. "A.J.'s Bail Bondman," I heard her say. "He's not here right now, but I can have him call you back." She added.

"How much is his bond?" Her questions continued. "With a bond that much, you guys are gonna need some type of collateral." She stated. "Okay, I'm gonna call him and have him call you back." She told the caller and then she hung up the phone.

But right when she was about to call Julian's cellphone, the front door opened, and he walked in. "I was just about to call you," Charmaine spoke first.

"What did I miss?" He asked her while he made his way towards me. I stood up from the lounge chair and embraced him after he opened his arms to me.

"A guy just called and said that he needed his brother bailed out," Charmaine replied.

"Tell me who doesn't need their brother bailed out?" Julian joked.

I chuckled too. I mean, he had a point. Who doesn't want to bail a family member out of jail?

"That was funny, right?" He asked me after he kissed me on the cheek.

I saw Charmaine grit on Julian and I after he kissed me and she wasn't a happy camper. "I got the brother's number if you want it." She pressed the issue.

"How much is his bond?" He wondered aloud after he let me go and walked towards Charmaine's desk.

"The brother says it's five hundred thousand."

Shocked by her response, I blurted out and said, "Five hundred thousand?"

"This brother must have money and collateral for this bond," Julian said to Charmaine.

"I told him that."

"And what did he say?"

"He said that he only had the ten percent, which is $50,000."

"That's not enough. With a bond like that I have to have at least one hundred dollars, a house for the collateral portion and two co-signers. Now if I can't get that, then he needs to call another bail bondsman."

"Are you gonna call him and tell 'em that?" Charmaine wanted to know.

"Isn't that what I have you for?"

"Yeah, but I told the guy that I was going to have you call him back."

"I don't care what you told him. So pick up the phone, call him back and tell him that I'm gonna need 100k, a house for collateral and two co-signers. Got it?"

"Yes, I got it." She replied sarcastically.

Seconds later, he turned his attention back to me and asked me if I was ready to leave. And after I told him I was, he grabbed me by the hand and escorted me to his car. I swear, I was so happy to get out of that place. Charmaine was about to pluck my last nerve.

The moment after we got in his car, I told him about the grueling conversation I had with Charmaine. He laughed at some of the things I said, but I quickly reminded him that it wasn't cool to have someone working with him that he used to play around in the bed with. He didn't think anything was wrong with it, especially if that part of that relationship was over. But when I switched the roles and asked him how he'd feel if I had my ex-boyfriend working for me, he saw my point. "I wouldn't like it at all." He admitted.

"So, tell me the last time you two had sex?" I pressed him.

"Want me to be honest?"

I punched him in his arm. “Of course, I want you to be honest.” I insisted.

“Okay, after I hired her to work for me, we had sex twice. But that’s it.” He confessed.

“And how long ago was that?”

“Like almost two years ago.”

“So, you fucked her twice right after you hired her? And it hasn’t happened since?” I probed him. I needed him to get this timeline straight because I’m too old for games. That little girl back at his office will make me kill her for sure.

“Yep. That’s about right.”

“Wait no, I don’t want to hear the *that’s about right* answer. Tell me how long it’s been since you two had sex?”

“Almost two years ago and it hasn’t happened since.”

“Are you sure?”

“Yes, I am sure.” He responded confidently and then he smiled.

“Don’t smiled at me.” I punched him once more in his arm. “You should’ve told me that you had your ex-girlfriend working for you.”

“You’re right, I should’ve told you. But, now it’s out and everything is all good, right?”

I rolled my eyes at him. “Don’t keep anything else from me, okay?”

“Okay, but wait.....” he said and then he paused, “It sounds like somcone is catching feelings.”

"I don't know who you're talking about." I folded my arms and turned my attention out of the passenger window.

"It's okay. You can tell me." He said jokingly.

"Nope, I'm not telling you anything. Now let's get to this restaurant. I'm hungry." I told him and played hard-to-get the rest of the way. Every other minute he'd reach over and tickle me. I thought it was cute and went with the floor.

What Else Could Go Wrong

My lunch date with Julian was awesome but it ended abruptly when he got yet another call to bail someone else out of jail. I was a bit disappointed but then I had to remember that this is his business and how he pays his bills, so I need to be a little more considerate. Nevertheless, the food was great, and I enjoyed his company, so I couldn't ask for me.

When we returned to his office, he dropped me off to my car and told me that he'd call me later. I told him that I'd be patiently waiting, we kissed and then I watched him as he drove off.

The second I took my eyes off his car, I looked at the front door of his office and what do you know, I catch Charmaine watching me from one of the side windows. But what was funny was that I caught her in the act. She didn't want me to see her staring at me, so that's why she jumped back from thc window. I shook my head and laughed and walked to my car.

Now the closer I get to my car; I see a white envelope tucked underneath my left windshield wiper. At first sight, I think it's a damn parking ticket and I instantly get pissed because where are the no fucking parking signs? But when I grabbed it, I looked at it closer and realized that it was a plain envelope with a note inside it. Before I pulled the note out of the envelope, I looked around my surrounding area to see if someone was watching me. And when I didn't see anyone acting out of the ordinary, I pulled the note out and unfolded it.

You need to call 757-555-1212 as soon as you get this msg. It read.

Suddenly, anxiety snuck back into my body and it began consuming me. I took another look around my surroundings and still, I found no one acting out of the ordinary. "Where the fuck are you?" I said underneath my breath as if I was trying to prevent someone from hearing me. Then it hit me, Charmaine had to have seen who left the note on my car that's why she was watching me from the office.

Without giving it, another thought I marched towards the office with the note in my hand. I found her silly ass sitting behind her desk when I walked in. "You guys are back," she said as if she was surprised to see me. I wanted to tell the bitch to cut the bullshit because I saw her watching me from the window. But then I asked myself, what for? She's gonna lie and then I'm gonna get mad and curse her out. So, the best course of action is to come in here and find out who left this fucking note on my car. That's it.

“I found this note on my car. Did you see who left it?” I asked her.

She quickly gave me a clueless expression. “No, I didn’t see anyone.”

“Well, did you see anyone hanging around my car?” I pressed her.

"No, I haven't."

"Are you sure?"

"Yes,"

I sighed heavily. "All right," I said and left without saying goodbye. I did call her a stupid bitch, which I'm sure she heard. And knowing this, I'm sure she's gonna tell Julian. But who cares? I've got more shit to worry about than her dingy ass.

I got back in my car with the note in hand, trying to decide if it would be a good idea to call this number. I also needed to decide whether or not to use my cellphone. I mean, what if this is the cops trying to set me up? And if that's the case, then I can't take that chance. I can't have the cops breaking down because I said something incriminating over the phone. No way. I can't make that sacrifice.

The drive back to my house came with its distractions. I tried to listen to my favorite song *You Are* by Charlie Wilson, I couldn't enjoy it because I couldn't get my mind off this freaking note. I need to find out who wrote it and more importantly why he or she wants to talk to me?

While mulling over the questions in my head, my cell phone rings, and it scares the shit out of me. I immediately look at my Bluetooth screen and realizes that the call was coming from my ex-husband, so I answered it on the second ring. “How can I help you?” I got straight to the point.

“I was calling to see how you were doing?”

“Bullshit! When have you ever cared about how I was doing?”

"My homeboy Eric told me that he saw you at the police station getting booked on a tampering with firefighting equipment charge. Then after he told me that, I'm watching TV and find out that Mariah's husband got killed while he was in the hospital. And I'm like, what's going on? It seems like every time I turn around someone is getting killed around here. Did he owe somebody money or something?"

“I can’t answer that. I didn’t fuck with William like that. I mean, I’m sorry that he was murdered, but in my mind, he got what he deserved, especially after the way he treated Mariah.”

“There you go on that scorn-bitter woman thing again.” He replied sarcastically.

“Trust me, I am not scorned or bitter. I am a very happy social butterfly and I credit my new man for that too.”

“Cut the shit! You’re in the honeymoon phase. It’s gonna all go up in smoke when he finds out how crazy you are.”

“Tell that to the hoes you’re sleeping with.”

"Don't concern yourself with me. I keep my hoes in check. Every one of them knows their place so later down the line, there won't be any misunderstandings."

"Everything that comes out of your mouth sounds like gibberish."

"That's because I won't tell you what you wanna hear."

"Look, I gotta go. Now have a fucked-up life." I told him and then I ended the call.

It didn't seem like it back then, but I am so happy that I divorced his adulterous ass. Fucker loser! Ugh!

I've gotta admit that I couldn't wait to get home. From the crazy-ass meeting, I had with my private investigator Mr. Tillman, the awkward meeting with Charmaine; Julian's office assistant and Rebound Bitch and the note left on my car drummed up a lot of chaos in my head. My problem now is how am I gonna handle it?

In the Arms of the Right Man

Later that night, Julian finally made his way back to my place. When he called my cell phone and told me that he was outside, I got out of bed, dragged myself to the front door and opened it so he could come in. "Do, you know what time it is?" I asked him as he stood before me in the foyer.

"You look sexy in that nightgown." He pointed out without answering my question.

"Don't get off the subject," I told him after I locked the front door and made my way down the hallway.

"Sweetheart, you know I wasn't trying to get off the subject." He replied as he followed me.

"Yeah, right," I commented as I entered my bedroom. The television was already powered on, so I handed Julian the remote control just in case he wanted to watch something else.

"Mind if I take off my clothes?" He asked while he stood at the edge of the bed.

"You know you can't get in my bed with them on," I replied sarcastically but in a jokingly manner.

"Yeah, that would make sense, huh?" He said with a smirk.

Instead of commenting, I smiled.

"So, I heard someone put a note on your car after I dropped you back off at my office."

I shook my head because I knew that noisy ass bitch was going to open her big mouth. "Yeah, they did," I replied nonchalantly.

"Did you ever find out who it was?" He probed me.

"Yes, I did." I lied, hoping he'd stop asking me questions.

"So, who was it?" His questions continued and then he crawled in my bed. He stripped down to his t-shirt and boxer briefs.

"Nobody important. Just some car detail service company flyer." I responded, trying to brush off the conversation altogether.

"You know what?"

"What?"

"I'm getting the sense that you don't wanna talk about it, so I'm gonna let it go."

"And you know what?"

"What?"

"I appreciate you doing that for me. So, thank you." I told him and then I leaned over and kissed him. "Will you hold me right now?" I changed the subject because what I needed was to be in his arms.

"Absolutely." He agreed eagerly and I didn't have to say another word to him. He completely took over after the first kiss. It went from passion to intoxication as he stuck his tongue inside of it. We kissed like two people in love. We rotated lips every two to three seconds and then he moved his lips off mine and began licking down my neck. I started squirming as the hot feeling in my loins caused me to wanna just grind my hips because my neck was my weak spot.

Julian pressed against me, and I could feel his rock-hard dick against my pelvis. I began grinding my hips upward towards his dick trying to press my clit on his rock-hard penis. I wanted him to know that I wanted to feel him inside of me really bad. Julian pulled my lace gown over my head and started rubbing my size C cup breasts with such passion. Before I knew it; my nipples were hard. They started pulsating as soon as he put his mouth on them. "Ohhh," I sang out. The heat from his mouth was sending me over the top. He sucked on my nipples so hard he caused me to grind harder and faster. I had to move my head side-to-side because it felt so good. Each time I moved, Julian sucked harder and harder. I couldn't control myself.

"I want you!" I screamed out.

My pussy was soaking wet. I could feel the moisture in my panties. He stood up abruptly and hovered over me. I looked up at him with innocent eyes. He quickly pulled off his boxer shorts and I immediately saw his erection. He slid my panties off next and the cool air on my clit made me feel hot as hell. I spread my legs open so Julian could get a good look at my creamy pussy. Any inhibitions I had previously about sleeping with him were gone.

"Damn, that is a pretty pussy! Mmmm, mmm," Julian complimented. I reached down and put my index finger in my pussy. I fingered my pussy, sliding my finger in and out, enticing him.

"Shit!" he moaned, grabbing his dick. Then he did some shit that surprised me. He dropped to his knees in front of me and put his face between my legs.

"Ahhh," I screamed out. Julian started darting his tongue into my hole real fast, in and out. "Oh God! Oh God! Oh God!" I hollered. My moans just drove him crazier. Julian made loud slurping noises while he ate the shit out of my pussy. I was pumping my ass, shoving that pussy at his tongue.

"C'mon . . . give it to me," I told him. His legs were toned, and his dick hung almost to his knees. I licked my lips, but before I could go down on him, he hoisted me up and held me against him. I put my legs up around his waist and straddled him. I held onto his neck so I wouldn't fall while he guided his dick into my pussy.

"Owww!" I screamed when he put his thick, solid dick inside of me. He flopped back on the couch, and now I was riding him. I bounced up and down on that dick so hard and fast he was breathing like he had just run laps. "Oh, fuck me! Fuck me good," I talked much shit while I rode that dick.

"Oh shit, girl, your pussy is out of this fucking world," Julian growled. Just when I thought he was going to cum, I jumped up off his dick.

"Wait...where you goin'?" he said, looking as if he was about to beg me to get back on it.

I laughed.

Then I turned around and got back on his dick backwards so he could see my whole ass, *the reverse cowgirl.* No man worth his salt could turn this shit down. Seeing a woman in this position made men's dicks harder and added to the throbbing sensation.

I bent over at the waist and pumped up and down on his dick again. "Awww fuck!" he moaned. Julian slapped my ass cheeks as I fucked the shit out of him. I planted my feet for leverage, and then I used both of my hands and spread my ass cheeks apart so he could see his dick go in and out of my pussy. "I see it! Fuck me! I see it!" He called out. This was what we women live for—to drive a muthafucka crazy tapping that ass. The ultimate in pussy whipping.

I started to feel myself about to cum because the shaft of his dick was pressing on my g-spot. "I'm coming!" I called out, and then I sat up, closed my legs together and squeezed his dick with my pussy.

"Agggghhhh!" Julian bucked and screamed. He was coming as well. I jumped up quickly, but I think some of his cum had got inside of me. I turned around, and he started jerking the rest of his cum onto my tits. That turned him on even more. "Goddamn girl, that was some bomb ass pussy,"

He gasped. He started rubbing his dick, and I watched it start to grow hard again.

"C'mere . . . we ain't finished yet," he said. Pulling me back down onto him, he and I went for rounds two, three and even, four. We finally collapsed from exhaustion. He kept telling me repeatedly how good my pussy was. I even remember him saying I was the best he ever had.

In the Blink of an Eye

Julian woke me up the following morning and told me that he had to leave because work was calling him. After he kissed me on the forehead, he promised me that I'd hear from him as soon as he gets a break. Not even five minutes after I locked my front door, my doorbell rings. I knew it was Julian coming back telling me that he left something, so I shouted at the front door and told him to hold on and that I was coming. "You can't stay away from me, huh?" I commented as I opened the door.

"Yes, I actually can't," a tall, black stocky guy replied as he stood at my front door.

Frighten by his appearance and stature, I wasn't sure of what to say to me, so I threw a generic question out at him. "Do I know you?" I asked politely.

"I left you a note on your car yesterday with my phone number on it, but you never called me." He replied. His words were polite, but his delivery wasn't. His voice was sinister like.

"I'm sorry about that. But the reason why I didn't call was because I thought someone was playing a prank on me." I lied but giving him the sincerest facial expression, I could muster up.

"I need to know whatcha' gon' do about Blue? He's in jail because he did a job for you." The guy replied in a menacing way. He kept direct eye contact too.

"But I paid him to do that job. I shouldn't have to get him out of jail." I tried to reason. But I responded in a nice and calm manner.

"Look, we don't give a fuck about that. My nigga is in jail and he got a bond of 500k, that means that he gotta have 100k in cash, somebody to put their house up for collateral and a cosigner."

"Hey, wait, did you call A.J.'s Bail Bondsman yesterday?"

"I called a lot of people. But no one wants to touch him. So, when me and my crew found out that you was fucking with that A.J, dude, we knew that all our problems will be solved."

"Wait… what?" I replied, trying to make sense of what he just said.

"You heard me. Either come up with the 100K, use your house as collateral or get your dude to get my dawg out. And if you don't then you gon' come up missing." He threatened me. I swear, I couldn't tell you how I felt after this guy told me that if I don't bail the hitman out of jail, then I'm gonna come up missing… I had a bunch of emotions. It even felt like my soul left my body too. I didn't know if I wanted to get on my knees and pray for my life. Or slam my door in his face and go hide in the back of my walk-in closet. Then I figured that both of those options wouldn't matter one bit, because I'd probably still end up dead. So, what's a girl to do?

"You got two days to get him out." The guy warned me and then he walked away.

Immediately after the guy walked away, I closed my front door and locked it. "Oh my God! What just happened?" I whispered, not realizing that I was home alone. But then I realized that that guy put so much fear in me that I almost forgot that I was home.

"Calm down Kim, relax. He's gone." I gave myself a pep talk after cautiously peering around the window treatment of my living room window.

Thankful that that asshole was gone, I was still spooked by his visit and the terms of his demand. I mean, why come to my home and threaten to take my life if I don't bail the hitman out of jail. I'm surprised that he even received a bond, especially after committing murder. It sounds like he already has a hook up down at the courthouse.

Afraid to come out of the house, I activated my security alarm, went into my bedroom, and climbed underneath the bedsheets with the door locked for extra security. But for some reason, hiding out in my bedroom didn't give me that safe feeling that I was looking for. I had to get out of this house. But where would I go? I don't have family that lives close to me. I can't go to the hospital to be with Mrs. Elaine. Tammy made sure of that. My ex-husband's club is out of the question. So, is Julian's office. I mean, how would I look hanging out at his office with that talkative ass Charmaine? That tramp would run me bananas with all that mouth she has. She talks nonstop all day long. She's noisy too. So, it didn't surprise me that she told Julian about the note left on my car. I know one thing; from this point on, I've got to keep her ass at arm's distance. It's evident that she's jealous of me and Julian's relationship, so she'll find anything to break us up.

I waited a couple of hours to make sure the coast was clear and then I strolled out of my house and headed to my car. I did this so that I could regroup and get a clear mind. Not only am I on the cop's radar and could possibly get charged for William's murder, I now have to come up with a get-out-of-jail free card for Blue. His homeboy has made it perfectly clear that if I don't then I will be murdered for sure. Now, what the hell am I going to do about that? I don't have that type of money. And I can't put my house up for collateral either. Is he fucking crazy? I would be a damn fool if I give away that type of money and put my house up. But let's just say that I do it, that bum could skip court and runoff in the sunset and I'd lose my money and my house. So, what do I do?

I drove under the speed limit until I got out of my neighborhood. I did this to make sure that I wasn't being followed. I guess I should've taken these same precautions before I came home after being arrested and going to Julian's office.

My car needed gas, so I stopped off at a gas station not too far from my house. I did the *look over my shoulder* thing to make sure that I hadn't been followed and then I started pumping the gas. Once I was done, I placed the hose back in the slot and then I headed in the convenient store. I wanted a pack of chewing gum, so I asked the Arab clerk behind the plexiglass partition to hand me the smallest box he had. He rung up the price of the gum, and as soon as I paid him, he handed it to me and then I left.

When I exited the corner store, I walked back to my car so I could get the hell out of dodge but one of Virginia Beach's finest delayed my plan. "Look at what we have here." Detective Miles said. He was leaning against the hood of my car.

"Can you get off my car, please?" I instructed.

"I see you're out on bail," he commented, smirking at me like he found something funny.

"Yeah, I see it too. Now get off my car." I replied sarcastically. I mean, who sits on another person's car?

He slid off the hood and stood up next to it as I approached him. "So, we hear that you stopped back by the hospital to see Mrs. Fisher. But the visit fell apart because Mrs. Slone got you escorted off the premises." He stated.

"Believe whatever you wanna believe," I said nonchalantly as I walked around to the driver's side door of my car.

"We also know that you had something to do with William Slone's murder. And as soon as I can prove it, you won't be walking around here as freely as you're doing now."

"Well, do your job then and stop harassing me," I told him.

"Adam Blue is gonna do the job for us. And before you know it, he's gonna cut a deal with us and turn states' evidence on your boogie ass."

"I don't know who that is." I brushed the name off.

"You can deny knowing him all you want, but you know Mrs. Fisher and once she finds out that you had her shot, she's gonna throw you to the wolves. I can guarantee you that."

"She wasn't supposed to be….." I said then I cut my words off in mid-sentence once I realized that I was about to implicate myself. I can't believe that he almost got me to confess to the hit. And what's insane about this, he heard me loud and clear.

"Hey, did you just say that she wasn't supposed to be there?" He asked me as he stood straight up, jogging his memory simultaneously.

"No, I didn't say that." I denied it, while trying to get in my car.

"Yes, you did. You just said that she wasn't supposed to be there." He said confidently. His manncrisms were that of a cop getting a confession from a suspect during an interrogation. But I didn't confess to anything. I will deny it to the very end.

Without saying another word, I got in the driver seat of my car, powered on the ignition and then I drove away slowly; to prevent him from pulling me over and giving me a speeding ticket. "I'm gonna take you down, Kim Weeks!" I heard him shout as I left the convenient store parking lot.

Once again, the cops found a way to ruffle my damn feathers. Where the hell did he come from? I was watching every mile I took, making sure I wasn't being followed. How did this happen? Then it hit me. I pulled my car over to the side of the road in a residential area and then I climbed out of my car. "Where you at GPS, I know you're somewhere underneath my car," I said after I walked around to the passenger side and got down on my knees.

I searched the front area of my tire and found nothing. Then I took a look under the passenger side door and still found nothing. But when I looked around the area of my back-right side of my tire, placed there in my face was a GPS tracker. Livid by the sight of it, I grabbed it and threw it onto the lawn of a home I had parked my car in front of. "You won't monitor anywhere else I drive to." I hissed.

Pissed off about the fact that my privacy was invaded, I sped off; squealing my tires on the streets in the residential neighborhood. I wanted to get as far as I could from that GPS tracker.

I Need an Ally

Thinking about the cops installing that GPS on my car infuriated me. I mean, they're that desperate to lock me back up that they'll stoop that low to harass me. Right now, I need an ally and the perfect person for that position is Mrs. Elaine. I need to get in her head and find out what she remembers the day she was shot. But before I do that, I need to make sure Tammy isn't anywhere around. If she is, then she'll derail my plans to speak with Mrs. Elaine. So, now is the time to make a drive-by at Tammy's house and pray to God that she's still there.

Taking the GPS off my car was a good thing, considering that I was going to Tammy's neighborhood. I can't have the cops swooping in on me like they're coming in to save the day. All I'm gonna do is check out the scenery and be on my way.

Now before I headed in the direction of the hospital, I stopped by a beauty supply store and purchased a wig. I knew I needed to disguise myself to prevent from being spotted at the hospital. With the wig in hand, I used the mirror underneath my sun visor to put it on correctly. I had to tug on it and push it back a few times until I had it right. Satisfied with my new look, I pushed the visor out of the way, started the ignition and then I sped off.

On this trip to the hospital, I felt confident that I was going to see Mrs. Elaine and we're gonna talk and then everything will go back to the way they were before the shooting. She loved me like I was her daughter, so I knew that there was no way that she was going to send me away. That's just not her.

I walked into the hospital from the outpatient side. I took the elevator up to the Intensive Care Unit and when I arrived on the floor, I held my head down slightly to keep from being noticed as I walked down the hallway towards Mrs. Elaine's room. Thankfully, no one recognized me so I felt a little optimistic about my visit with Mrs. Elaine. Immediately after I stepped up to the door of her room, I tapped on it lightly and said, "Mrs. Elaine, it's me Kim and I'm coming in." I announced in a reasonable tone to keep the nurses roaming around the hallway from hearing me, but I also said it loud enough for Mrs. Elaine to hear me.

After I pushed the door open and walked into the room, I was greeted by two of Mrs. Elaine's family members while she laid there in her bed. Her eyes lit up when she saw me. "Hi baby, I've been trying to contact you." She told me.

I walked up to her bed, leaned in and hugged her. "I'm so glad you're doing better." I pointed out.

"You're such a sweetheart. And what did you do to your hair? Did you color it?"

"It's a wig."

"It's different, but it fits you." She replied and then she introduced me to the two women sitting the chairs on the left side of her bed. "Kim, to my left is my oldest sister Mary. And that pretty little thing sitting next to her is my niece Pam. They came all the way down here to see me."

"Nice to meet you both," I said and smiled. Mrs. Elaine's and her sister looked like twins. Her niece Pam was a cute and very athletic looking girl. She resembled the female boxer, Laylah Ali.

"She was Mariah's best friend before she passed." Mrs. Elaine told them.

"Oh, you're the one that found my cousin hanging in your house?" The chick Pam asked.

Thrown off by the question, I paused for a bit and then I answered her, "Unfortunately, yes." Then I shifted the conversation in another direction, "So how are you? I was worried about you after I got the call. I was here waiting for you while they were performing your surgery but then something happened, and I had to leave."

"Yes, Tammy told me."

"So, where are the girls?" I asked, trying to stay away from talking about Tammy.

"Tammy has them." She replied.

As hard as I tried to stay away from speaking Tammy's name, Mrs. Elaine brings it up again.

"Have you seen them since you've been here?"

"Yes, Tammy brought them by earlier."

"How are they?"

“They’re doing great. As soon as they saw me, they started asking a bunch of questions about why I was here. So, I told them that I got sick and the doctor had to fix me up. You know, kids are so inquisitive.” Mrs. Elaine chuckled.

"You're right about that," I commented. "So, has the cops talked to you about the shooting since you've been in recovery?" I asked. I tried to pick my words carefully since I was in the company of Mrs. Elaine's sister and niece.

She let out a long sigh. “Yes, they have. I didn’t want to say anything to you about it because they told me not to talk to you.”

“Really? Why?” I responded sympathetically. I needed to sound like I was on Mrs. Elaine and the cops’ side.

"They said that they got the guy who shot me and William, so I was relieved when they told me that. But then right after they told me that, they came up with this insane story that you had something to do with it. And I told them that that can't be right. You wouldn't dare try to have me killed. For heaven's sack you were a part of my family; my daughter's best friend." she defended me.

“Absolutely, not!” I interjected.

"Listen, honey, the police always have their own theories. So, just let the chips fall where they may." She encouraged me.

“Has the doctor told you when they’re gonna release you?” I changed the subject once again. I could feel the hard, cold stares coming from Mrs. Elaine's niece.

"No, not yet."

"Do you need anything?" I wondered aloud.

"No sweetheart, I'm fine." Mrs. Elaine replied.

"Well, since you have your family here with you, I'm gonna head out. But if you need anything and I mean anything, give me a call." I insisted and then I leaned over and kissed her on the cheek.

"I love you, sweetheart! Be careful out there."

"Don't worry, I will," I assured her as I backed away from her bed.

"Can I speak to you for a moment?" Her niece Pam asked me.

Shocked by her request, I paused and then I said, "Yes, sure. Let's go."

Without saying a word, Pam followed me into the hallway and closed the door to Mrs. Elaine's room immediately thereafter. I sized her up from head to toe, to examine whether or not I would be able to take her down if she tries to attack me. I mean, she was gritting on me the entire time I was visiting Mrs. Elaine. I wondered what her deal was.

"What's up?" I asked her.

"There's no secret how much my aunt loves you, but for me, something doesn't feel right." She pointed out.

"What do you mean by that?" I questioned her, not sure where this conversation was going.

“My mother and I talked to Tammy and she told us that she knows you had something to do with my niece’s father’s murder.”

Flushed by her accusation, my body filled up with heat and it felt like my blood was boiling on the inside. “That bitch is crazy. She’s just trying to put everybody against me because she didn’t like Mariah.” I started off saying. I knew it was important to put Tammy in a dark light. “She’s the reason why Mariah arrested and hit with a protective order.”

"Look, I'm not sure about what happened with that situation, but what I do know is that you set off the fire alarm on another floor of this hospital and while the alarm was going off, William and my auntie get shot."

"I didn't set off the alarm," I said sharply.

"Okay, listen, you can deny it all you want, my reason for talking to you is to tell you that my mother and I want you to stay away from my aunt until the police clear you of all wrongdoings."

"Does Mrs. Elaine know that you're telling me this?" I wanted to know. I mean, how dare you keep me away from my best friend's mother. I loved Mrs. Elaine and I'd do anything for that lady. So, to have this damn chick tell me to stay away from her is like a slap in the face. One part of me wants to go back into the room and tell Mrs. Elaine what her niece is trying to make me do. But since there's a lot of shit going on and I don't want to cause a scene, I'm gonna leave it alone.

"I'm gonna tell her when I go back into the room." She told me.

Annoyed by this whole thing, I refused to say another word in my defense, so I threw my hands up and then I stormed off.

By the time I reached my car, I realized that even though Mrs. Elaine's family doesn't want me around, Mrs. Elaine still thinks of me as her daughter and she's convinced that I had nothing to do with her getting shot. Hearing that was like music to my ears. Now, all I gotta do is work on Julian. Who knows how that is going to work out? I guess I will find out.

Later that evening I got a call from Julian telling me that he may not stop by my place tonight; saying, there was a tailgating party at one of the local universities that got out of hand so he's gonna be busy bailing a lot of people out of jail. I told him that I understood and that I'd see him the following day.

Another GPS Tracker

I was sound to sleep when my doorbell rang. When I looked at the time on my cable box and realized that it was a little after 2 a.m. I knew it was no one but Julian. I dragged myself out of the bed and headed to the front door. "I'm coming," I shouted as I soon as I was five hundred feet away from the front door. Immediately after I approached it, I opened it slowly to give the impression that I wasn't being thirsty because he was here. During my marriage, I treated my ex-husband like a king. He was my everything and at times he made me feel desperate in ways that I'd pursue him more than he did me—in the bedroom was at the top of the list.

Startled and consumed with fear by the tall, stocky figure standing at my feet door made me react by trying to slam my front door shut. But I couldn't do it. I wasn't strong or fast enough. "Somebody help!" I yelled while trying to hold the guy at bay.

“Yo' get off the door and stop screaming before I kill yo' ass!” He threatened me as he put more of his body weight against the front door.

“Who are you? What do you want?”

“I'm the guy from earlier so get off the fucking door.” He roared.

Somehow feeling better because the guy trying to burst into my place admitted to being the guy I spoke to earlier gave me a sense of relief. The other thing that stopped me from being resistant was that he threatened to kill me. I'll say and do whatever I have to do to stay alive so I released the door. He crossed over the threshold of my front door but he didn't walk further than that. "Why you take the GPS off your car?" Was his first question.

Shocked by his question, I said, “That was you? I thought it was the cops.”

"Nah, it was me. I put it up there to make sure you don't try to leave town before you do what you're supposed to do." He explained. "Where you at with that anyway?" He wanted to know.

"I'm still working on it," I said.

“You know you only got 24-hours left right?”

I felt a large lump in my throat after he reminded me of how much time I had left to come up with the hitman's bail money and collateral. "Yeah, I know," I said reluctantly.

“I don’t like the sound of that.” He pointed out. “You’re gonna have to be a little more enthusiastic than that.” He added as he towered over me.

“Think I could get a little more time? Like another week? I know I could work something out by then.” I suggested. I really needed more time to figure out how I’m gonna get myself out of this jam. With the cops on my back and having to deal with Tammy and Mrs. Elaine’s family is a bit much for me to handle all at once.

“Nah, you got 24 hours. That’s it. Now if you don’t come through with what we asked for, then we’re gonna get rid of that old lady in the hospital, those two little girls and then we’re gonna come after you.” He replied and he was adamant.

I stood there and didn't say another word. All I could do was think about was how my life was going to end in 24 hours. Who would've thought that the couple of women I had killed, I'd be on my way to see them again in the afterlife? I guess what that say is true, *you live by the sword, you die by the sword.*

"Your ex-husband owns that night club right?" He asked me.

“Yeah, why?”

"I heard he was big time. He buys and sells a lot of big shit. Shit that he can get a large return on. People on the street say that he's a loan shark too. So get the dough from him?" He suggested.

“I don’t fuck with him like that. We’re not even on speaking terms. And even if we were, he wouldn’t give me that type of money. We hate each other’s guts.”

"Well, I don't know what to tell you. You got 24 hours as I said before. So, I'll see you then." He said.

"What's your name?"

"Just call me the driver." He continued and then he left.

I closed my front door as soon as he walked away. My nerves were all over the place. At one point, I thought he was trying to kill me. Then to find out that he was only here to make sure that I don't take off the new GPS device he just stuck on my car. But what was really, odd was the idea he gave me about getting the money from Drake. I know Drake would laugh me off the phone if I asked him for that kind of money. It wouldn't matter if I visited him in person and told him what was going on and that I needed the money to stay alive. Knowing him, he'd be happy to see someone take me out. As far as he's concerned, I could be here today and be gone tomorrow and he wouldn't care.

I tried to go back to sleep after the guy left my place, but I kept tossing and turning the rest of the night. And the one thing I couldn't stop thinking about was the idea of robbing my ex-husband. The more I thought about it, the more a plan started formulating. By sunrise, it hit me. Instead of asking Drake for the money, I could get the hitman's people to rob him.

Now I had no earthly idea that Drake was involved in buying and selling stolen goods. I would've never guessed that he was a loan shark either. The one thing I did know was that he kept large sums of money in the safe at his night club. So, if he's into all those unsavory business dealings, then it's likely that he's got a minimum of at least fifty-grand in his safe and that is on a slow night. On a good night, Drake could have one-hundred and fifty thousand tucked away. That's not to say that he'd give up the money easily. He's gonna give the hitman's people a run for his money. Someone is gonna end up dead. Hopefully, it's Drake because if he lives, he's gonna find out who set up the robbery. He's just that connected in the streets; being a night club owner and all.

While ironing out the pros and cons of the robbery, I remembered that I'd inherit Drake's night club and I could cash in on his insurance policy per our divorce decree. All seven hundred and fifty thousand of it. Yep, I took that policy out on him four years ago still get billed for it until this day. I remember getting it when I started seeing our marriage going down in the drain. If I play this right, the hitman would get out of jail, my husband would be pushing up daisies and I'll be cashing in on a heathy insurance policy. This will be a win-win for all parties involved. But the hitman and his people will have to give me more time to orchestrate this plan.

Ten hours after that guy left my house, I grabbed the burner phone from my purse and used it to dial the number the guy wrote on the note that was left on my car a couple of days prior. He answered it on the second ring. "Who dis?" He asked. His voice definitely sounded like a nigga from the hood.

“This is Kim,” I said, not knowing what else to say.

"You got some good news for me?" He asked me.

"Yes, as a matter of fact, I do. Not sure if you want to discuss it over the phone." I pointed out.

"Want me to come by your spot?"

“No, but I could meet you at the Mc. Donald’s not too far from my house.” I suggested.

“Why I can’t come to your crib?”

“Because I have noisy neighbors.”

“That’s not a good enough answer. I’ll be at your house in 30 minutes.”

I sucked my teeth. I didn't want this guy to keep popping up at my house. What if the cops are watching me? I had almost blown my cover with the shooting at the hospital. So, it's very important that I keep my circle tight. No more mix-ups. "All right," I said and then I ended the call.

The guy who told me to call him the driver came back as he stated. He didn't have to knock on the door when he arrived at my front door, because I kept watch out for him from my living room window. "Come on in," I instructed.

"Nah, I prefer you to come to my car. That way I ain't gotta worry about if your house is wired or something."

“My house isn’t wired.”

"Sorry, but I ain't gonna take that risk so follow me." He demanded.

By the look on this guy's face, I knew that he wasn't taking no for an answer. It was either I walk to his car or he was going to leave. I couldn't let that happen because I needed him and his crew to execute the robbery. If they don't do it, then I won't be able to get the money that's being extorted from me, so I reluctantly followed the guy to his car. In route to the car, I looked over my shoulders in all directions. I needed to make sure that I wasn't being watched by the cops.

When we arrived at the car, I was instructed to get in the back seat of a black, late-model Dodge Charger. The windows were completely tinted black and there was no way someone from the outside would be able to see inside this vehicle. After I climbed in the back seat, I was greeted by a guy in the front passenger seat and a guy in the back seat sitting next to me. I spoke to both men but no one replied. "Tell us what's on your mind?" The driver said.

"Remember you brought the idea of me asking my ex-husband for the money?"

"Yeah," he replied.

"Well, I've come up with a plan. And it's gonna make you guys a lot of money."

"Tell us about it," he instructed me.

"Okay, so here's the deal. If I go to my ex-husband for the money, he's gonna make a spectacle of me and laugh me out of his nightclub, so I think the best plan for all parties involved is for you guys to rob him."

Everyone besides me burst into laughter. "She's a firecracker, huh?" the driver asked the other two.

Neither one responded. They nodded their heads instead.

"Now how do you propose we do that? We just can't run up in that man's establishment and demand money?" the driver's questioned.

"My ex keeps his money in a safe under his desk. There's an app on his smartphone that activates after he enters in a five-digit code. Once that code is activated, the desk in his office will move forward and the safe will appear. When we were together, he sometimes collected one hundred thousand on a slow day." I embellished a bit. When in reality, he'd only have half of that amount. "But now that he's into more illegal dealings I'm sure he'll have way more than that. As a matter of fact, it wouldn't shock me if he has more."

"You still haven't told us how we're gonna get the dough." The driver reminded me.

"He closes the club at 2 a.m. so you guys will have to go there and scope out everything like an hour before he closes the door."

"If that nigga is holding that kind of dough inside his club, he's gotta have muscle."

"He has three guys that does his security. So, they'll be easy to eliminate. Just take them out first." I suggested.

"You make it sound so easy." The driver said.

"Because it is."

"That spot got metal detectors at the front door." The guy in the back seat sitting next to me finally spoke.

I turned my attention towards him. "So, you can talk, huh?" I said sarcastically.

"Yeah, he's right. That spot does have a metal detector." The driver agreed and then he looked at me. "For this shit to work, you're gonna have to walk us in that spot." He said.

A ton of different emotions engulfed me. "No way, I can't do that."

"Why not?" the driver wanted to know.

"Because it'll never work. As soon as he sees me, he's gonna know something is up."

"It's either that or nothing because I ain't sending my soldiers in that spot unarmed. They'll get slaughtered.

I thought for a minute, trying to figure out how I could maneuver things if I escort these guys into Drake's club. But I couldn't come up with a logical reason when Drake ask me why I'm at his club that time of that night. He's gonna know something isn't right. "It's not gonna work. He knows me inside and out. He's gonna know something is up." I protested.

"That's not the answer I wanted to hear. And now that you're wasting my time, get the fuck out of my car and figure out another way to get hitman's bail money. Remember he needs 100k, a house for collateral and two cosigners. His girlfriend will sign, and you will be the other person signing his bail. That is if you go through another bondsman. If you use your boyfriend, then I'm sure he'll do it for free." The driver roared. He unleashed venom when he spoke to me.

Realizing that he wasn't playing games with me, I reconsidered and agreed to escort them into Drake's club; but under one condition. "What's the condition?" The driver wanted to know.

"You gotta kill my ex-husband before anyone exits the club," I told him. But I wasn't going to tell him that I would inherit the night club or cash in on a $750,000.00 insurance payout. No way! These guys would kill me for sure.

"Oh, that's easy. That's what we do." The driver admitted and then chuckled. The other two buys in the car laughed too. "So, when are we going in there?" He wanted to know.

"I was thinking like, two to three days from now."

"Fuck Nah! If we ain't going tonight, then it's gotta be tomorrow night."

"All right, then tomorrow night." I compromised.

"Cool. Well, I'll get with you tomorrow. Now don't do anything stupid until then." The driver insulted me.

"You either," I replied sarcastically and then I opened the back door and got out of the car.

As the car drove away, I saw another car driving towards me through my peripheral vision. The color was recognizable and the way the drill looked, sparked my curiosity, so I turned and looked over my shoulder and who do I see? My night in shining armor. I smiled at him and watched as he parked his car alongside the curb in front of my house, and then I walked over to greet him.

"Whose black car was that?" He asked me after he climbed out the driver seat of his car with two cups of Starbucks coffee in his hand.

"That was my best friend's brother coming by to check on me. He lives out of town, so he wanted to drop by and bid his farewell." I lied. I swear I have no idea how quickly I came up with that story. I'm good.

Julian smiled at me and then he kissed me on the cheek. "For a moment there, I thought it was your side boyfriend."

"Oh no, I wouldn't dare," I assured him as we headed towards my house.

"You better not." He commented.

I'm Losing My Mind

The next morning, Julian woke me up to breakfast in bed. He found the brand-new food tray I received as a Christmas gift six months back from Mariah. Julian had the tray plated with a Belgium waffle, four strips of turkey bacon and a side of scrambled eggs with cheese. The food looked absolutely wonderful. "Oh my God! Thank you so much, honey!" I thanked him as I sat up on the bed with my back rested against the headboard.

"Looks good, huh?" he asked as he placed the tray on my lap while I was tucked away underneath the bed comfortable.

"Yes, it does," I assured him while I contemplated on which dish, I was going to put in my mouth first. "Baby, I don't know what to eat first." I whined a bit like a big ole' baby.

"Try the eggs first. I cook the best eggs." He bragged.

"Okay, let me see," I said as I poked the eggs with my fork. I had to gather the eggs with just the right amount of cheese and when I saw that I had done that, I put the forkful of food in my mouth. "Hmmm, oh yeah, baby, these eggs are delicious."

"I told you." He smiled. But then his cell phone shifted his attention. It started chirping so he grabbed it from the lampstand on the right side of my bed.

I continued to eat my food while he went through his phone. I even grabbed the remote control from the lampstand on the side of my bed and powered on the television. I sifted through the channels and finally decided to watch the Wendy William's talk show. I loved that show because it was always entertaining.

"Hey, babe, doesn't your ex-husband own that night club on Bush Street?" he started off saying, so I turned my focus to him.

“Yes, why?” I asked him.

"Because the local news is reporting that it caught on fire last night."

"What?" I rasped, clutching the collar area of my shirt. In my head, I'm hoping that this news wasn't true.

Julian handed me his cellphone so I could read the article on my own. The title of the article was *Local nightclub set on Fire*:

Firefighters were called to Trinity nightclub in the Tidewater area at 2:36 a.m. Firefighters had to work to access an enclosed space in the building to put out the fire. No one was inside the building when the fire started. Firefighters said the flames were contained to that enclosed space and part of the building's exterior. Shortly after the fire was out, the fire investigators said they were investigating the fire as possibly being suspicious. The club has surveillance cameras outside the night club, but the fire marshal isn't sure if they captured the culprits and what happened moments before the fire was set. We spoke to the club owner not too long ago and he said that what happened was truly unfortunate, but he will work diligently to get the necessary renovations to get the night club back up and running.

Feeling sick to my stomach that the plans to rob my ex-husband's night club have gone up in smoke. What am I going to do now? The hitman's people aren't gonna give me a break because we can't pull off the heist tonight. What they will do is give me their ass to kiss and then put a bullet through my skull. So, what am I going to do now?

"That's a bummer, right?" Julian asked me after I handed him his cell phone back.

"Yes, it is," I replied, while my stomach filled up with knots of anxiety. I lose my appetite several seconds later.

"Are you all right?" He asked me after I removed the food tray from my lap and sat it on the bed next to me.

I wanted to tell him no I wasn't and what I had planned to do to Drake's place tonight. But I couldn't because he wouldn't understand, and I believe that he will look at me differently. I used to be this heartbroken woman because of an ex-husband that abused me mentally and emotionally. And because of this hurt, I became vengeful and wanted everyone that played a part in it to suffer with their lives. But now that Julian has come in my life, I feel loved again and I no longer want to hurt the women Drake was involved with. I say, let

God handle them. Let him punish them the way he sees fit. Drake too.

“Yes, I am.” I finally said.

"I'm finding a hard time believing that," Julian stated as he moved closer to me on the bed.

"I'm sorry. But I need to go." I told him and then I slid off my bed. Julian sat on the bed and watched me as I grabbed garments of clothing from my dresser drawers. "Are you leaving?" He wanted to know.

"Yes, I've got to go," I replied and headed into my bathroom shower. Immediately after I turned the shower water on, I grabbed my shower cap, got undressed and then I hopped into the shower. Midway through the shower, Julian popped his head into the bathroom and told me that he had to leave. "Lock the front door from the inside before you close the door," I instructed him.

“Will do.” He said and then he left.

The Deal Breaker

I had tunnel vision from the moment I found out that Drake's night club caught on fire. I also had reservations about talking to hitman's boy about it. But I knew that it was a conversation to be had. If not, he'd come looking for me and murder Mrs. Elaine and those innocent little girls like he warned me.

Once I was dressed, I grabbed my burner phone, handbag, and car keys and headed out the front door. Unbeknownst to me, I didn't have to travel far, because the hitman's liaison met me in front of my house. "On your way somewhere?" He asked me. I hadn't noticed before, but this guy was extremely huge. His statue alone resembled Suge Knight. His skin complexion was just a little darker.

"I was getting ready to call you," I told him, while we both stood a few feet from my front door.

"I hope it was about your ex's night club."

"Yeah, that's the conversation I was calling you to have."

"So, what are we going to do now?" He wanted to know. He didn't look too happy about the change in plans.

"I was wondering if we could wait until he gets the club's renovations done. By then, he'll have more money because he's gonna collect an insurance check."

"Nah, that's not gonna fly. You got until tonight to come up with the dough and the collateral. If you don't then, you, your best friend's mother and the grandkids will get a couple of slugs in the head. Do I make myself clear?"

“Yes,” I said.

“Don’t try to leave town.” He warned me and then he walked away.

Panic-stricken and confused, I just stood there and watched the guy walk away from me. "What the hell have you gotten yourself into Kim? This has got to be a nightmare." I said aloud, hoping that I'd wake up. But when I pinched myself in the arm, I realized that I wasn't asleep. What I'm going through is, in fact, real, so I better think of a way to get out of it. And do it by the end of the night.

Instead of going back into the house, I got in my car and drove in the direction of Julian's office. I knew I was against telling him about my dilemma, but now I don't have any other options. I figure that if I tell him how much trouble I was in without telling him that I put every one of Drake's mistresses on the chopping block, he'd want to save my life by getting the hitman out of jail. Now if he doesn't help me, then I will know exactly where we stand.

During my drive to his office, I tried calling him a couple of times, but he didn't answer.

"Please, be at work," I uttered to myself. If he wasn't there, then that means that I'm gonna must track him down and I needed all the time I could get.

The drive to his office took approximately eighteen minutes, which wasn't a long time on a normal day, but with what I had on my chest, it seemed like forever. Thankfully, I saw his car parked in the parking lot, because if it wasn't there then I'd be a basket case for real.

When I walked through the front door, Charmaine ass was front and center and she looked like she wasn't doing shit behind that desk. "Good morning." She greeted me.

"Good morning to you too, where is Julian?" I replied.

"He told me to tell you that he's on a very important call and that he'll call you later." He explained and then she gave me this stupid ass smirk on her face. It felt like she enjoyed every word she uttered.

Instead of feeding into her bullshit antics, I stormed towards this office and as soon as I reached the door, I opened it and walked right in. Contrary to what Charmaine said, he wasn't on the phone. In fact, he looked like he was shocked to see me. "We need to talk." I didn't hesitate to say after I closed his office door behind me.

"Why aren't you with your ex-husband? You ran out of your house to be by his side after you found out that his night club caught fire."

“Baby, I didn’t rush out of the house to go and see him, I did it for another reason.”

“Do you care to elaborate?” He asked.

"It's really complicated," I replied as I walked towards him.

“You might be making it more complicated than it is.”

“I know I may be asking you this prematurely, but do you love me?” I asked him after I walked around his desk and stood up directly in front of him.

“Do you love me?” He threw the question back at me.

“Yes, I do.”

"Well, then I love you too," he admitted while sitting in his chair while I towered over him.

"Do you love me enough to save my life if you had the resources to do it?" My questions continued.

“Yes, of course,” he assured me.

"Well, I'm about to say something and I don't want you to be mad with me. All I need from you right now is your support." I began to explain by giving him full disclosure.

“Kim, tell me what’s going on?” He insisted.

I took a deep breath and then I exhaled, only to come up with a plausible story that he’d believe since I couldn’t tell him the real story. “When I was married to Drake, he and I borrowed money to get the night club. We've paid them on time every month for the past couple of years, but after our divorce was final, he hasn't been paying them. So, when I saw that the club caught on fire, I knew that it had something to do with the money. Fast forward to yesterday, that car you saw me getting out of was one of the guy's coming to collect. But I don't have that kind of money. Drake has the money."

"How much do you and Drake owe those guys?"

“Remember the phone call Charmaine got the other day when a guy called and said that he needed to get his brother bailed out of jail and you said that he needs to come up with one hundred thousand dollars, collateral and two co-signers?”

“Yes, I remember.”

“Well, that’s the same guy that drove away from my house yesterday.”

"So, let me get this straight. You and your ex-husband owe a lot of money to a guy that's in jail and now the guy wants you to bail him out because you and your ex don't have the money?"

“Julian, they know that you and I are together. Since I couldn’t come up with the money, they basically want you to waive the entire amount of money that would be required and the collateral portion as well.”

Julian sat there and looked at me long and hard. Several seconds later, he pushed me away from him.”

“I can’t believe that this is happening to me.”

Stunned by the fact that he just pushed me away from him was a pill that was hard to swallow. I immediately got choked up. “What was that for?” I asked him as tears began to form in my eyes.

“Just leave Kim. Leave my office now.” He spat. I knew he was pissed.

“They said that they’re gonna kill me if I don’t come up with the money or get you to get ‘em out of jail.”

“That’s not my problem. So, what you need to do is get Drake on the phone and somehow come up with a resolution because I don’t have any dogs in that fight. All that shit you just told me has nothing to do with me so I’m not carrying that baggage with you.”

“But you said that you loved me.” I reminded him while the tears fell from my eyes.

"Kim, just leave, please. I refuse to listen to this nonsense." He said and then he stood up from his office chair and left me standing in his office alone. A few seconds later, I ran down behind him. But the time I made it to the reception area, where Charmaine was, Julian had already gotten outside. So, I made a run for it with hopes to catch up with him. I was too late though. By the time I reached the area where his car was parked, he had already driven away.

Knowing that I only had hours of life to live on this earth, I stood there and let the floodgates open. I began crying uncontrollably. "What am I gonna do now?" I asked myself through the sniffles.

My Last Straw

Not having too many options of people to call or places to go, I figured the only person left that I could talk to was my private investigator, Mr. Tillman. Now he and I had to go through that rough patch the last time I was at his office, but I'm more than sure that he's got himself together after I threatened to tell the cops that he was in on the murders too. Armed with all of this, I know Mr. Tillman will welcome me with open arms so I hopped back in my car and drove straight to his office.

When I pulled up to Mr. Tillman's office building, I felt optimistic that he was going to help me come up with a solution to my problem. And while I was there, I figured why not get my files in the process, just in case shit hits the fan. I can't have the cops finding the names of the women that have recently been murdered. I don't want that connection revealed because I'd never see the light of day if that happened. The hitman wouldn't either.

Still upset about the way things ended with Julian, I tried to brush those feelings off my shoulders so I would be clearheaded when I have this talk with Mr. Tillman. Mr. Tillman was the typc of man that would out-talk you if you let him. That meant to stay on your toes at all times.

I rehearsed over and over in my head what would be appropriate to tell Mr. Tillman without scaring him off like Julian did. I can only hope that everything goes well because I only have hours left until I have to pay up.

Dreading to walk down this long hallway to get to Mr. Tillman's office, I stopped midway and decided to use the ladies' restroom. I had been holding my bladder the entire day it seemed like. I believed that if I didn't go, I was sure to use the bathroom on myself.

Now while I was on the potty, I heard gunshots. I heard three gunshots in all. BOOM! BOOM! BOOM! I froze while I was in the middle of peeing. I even held my breath because I didn't want my presence to be known. Seconds later, I heard two sets of footsteps. They ran right by the bathroom door. "Hurry up!" I heard a male's voice say.

"I'm coming," I heard another male's voice say as he ran by the bathroom door. I swear, my mind was working overtime. I was also fearful of what was going on which was why I stood up slowly from the toilet stool. Somehow, I didn't have to use the bathroom anymore. My main concern was to get out of this fucking building.

After I pulled up my pants, I walked to the bathroom door slowly and then I pulled the door open. While it was slightly ajar, I peered my head around the door to see if I saw anyone and when I didn't, I walked out of the bathroom as quickly as I could.

Now I'm back in the hallway, and I have no idea what to do. Should I leave the building all together or should I check to see if anyone on this floor was hurt? "Come on Kim, just check to see if things are all right." I coached myself. I needed to build up the courage to move forward.

Finally, my walk to Mr. Tillman's office had come to an end. I pushed the door open to walk into the reception area and immediately after I walked across the threshold, I didn't see Mr. Tillman's office assistant anywhere. "Is anyone here?" I shouted. But I got no answer.

"Mr. Tillman are you in here?" I shouted once again. This time I walked towards this office. "Mr. Tillman where are you?" I yelled as I approached the door to his office. Once again, I didn't get an answer. So, I opened his door. "Mr. Tillman, it's Kim, I'm coming in," I announced. But I still didn't get an answer. I looked around his office from the doorway to locate his file cabinet since no one was around to help me secure my files. "There you go," I said after zooming in on the cabinet that was placed next to his desk. At that moment, I dashed towards the file cabinet and as soon as it was within arm's distance of me, I pulled each drawer out until I located my file. But after going through every file in there, my file was nowhere to be found. "Shit! Where the fuck is my file?" I spat. I was getting irritated by the second. "Wait, its gotta be in or on his desk." I wondered aloud and as soon as I turned around to search Mr. Tillman's desk, he was standing at the entryway to his office door. Startled, I said, "Where were you? I called your name about five times."

“Why are you in my office, going through my things?”

“I was looking for my file?”

“Get away from there.” He instructed me. “Just get out of my office altogether. And where is Claire? She knows better than to let anyone in my damn office."

"She wasn't here when I got here. So, I came back here looking for you and when you didn't answer I kinda let myself into your office." I explained as I gave him a cheap smile.

Mr. Tillman stormed away from his office door after I walked away from his desk. "Claire where are you?" He shouted and then I heard a gasping sound. "What the fuck!" He yelled.

Wanting to see why Mr. Tillman yelled, I ran back down the hallway towards the reception area of the front of the office and found Mr. Tillman holding Claire in his arms. She was bleeding from her mouth. I saw a lot of blood coming from her chest area too. It was apparent that she was dead. I guess now, I know who was struck with those three bullets.

“Call the paramedics.” Mr. Tillman snapped. “Call ‘em now,” he added.

"Call 'em and say what? She's already dead." I told him.

"Did you do this to her?" He questioned me as he gritted his teeth.

"Fuck no! Are you crazy?" I barked at him.

"Well, I believe you did." He pressed the issue and then he grabbed his cell phone from his pants pocket and dialed 911.

"Well if you believe I did it, then you know where I live. Send the cops there and tell 'em I'll be there waiting on them." I said. The only reason I encouraged Mr. Tillman to send the cops to my door, was because I was going to need somewhere to stay tonight, where I am being watched over 24-7. Allowing the cops to take me to jail will give me another day of life until I can figure out my next move.

Once again, I had no place to go, so I went home. I also decided to go home because I knew that Mr. Tillman was going to send the cops there to arrest me. And before I let that happen, I needed to get rid of all the documents and photos I had of all the women Drake screwed around with. I burned every single thing I had that could link me to those whores. I figured I had to be smart and take every precaution to cover up my misdeeds. The other stuff I wasn't too concerned with because my hands weren't dirty. When the cops come to my house to talk to me about Mr. Tillman's office assistant's murder and do their investigative stuff, they're gonna quickly realized that I didn't pull the trigger that killed her and then they're gonna let me go.

Anything outside of that, I'd be fucked for real. That's why I'm doing this sweep through my house now. I can't afford to slip up and let those crackers catch me with my pants down. I refuse to give them that satisfaction.

Less than thirty minutes later, the cops showed up. They read me my right and they told me what I was going to be charged with, but I let it go through one ear and out the other one. I wasn't fazed by any of this bullshit! I only allowed things to go down like that so I could buy myself some time. Fucking dummies!

Couldn't Believe My Eyes

"Inmate Weeks, you have an attorney visit," a female Correctional Officer shouted.

I climbed down from the top bunk in my cell, slipped on my correctional issued orange jumpsuit and Ked tennis shoes and then I headed towards the Exit Door. After I approached the door to the main cell block, the white, female C.O. asked me to show her my wristband so I did and when she validated that I was the inmate she came for, she unlocked the door and let me out.

"Stay on the white line at all times until I tell you otherwise, understood?" She instructed me.

I gave her a head nod.

The walk to the visiting room was about three hundred feet so I got there fairly quickly. "We're going through this door." She pointed out so I could move to the left side of her. After I stepped to the side, she unlocked and opened the heavy steel door, she instructed me to sit in the second phone booth. "Your attorney will be with you shortly so stay seated there until I come back and get you." She added.

"Okay, thanks," I replied and then she left. I sat down on the metal seat and waited for an attorney to show up and talk to me from the other side of the glass partition. I even wondered who it could be because I hadn't hired an attorney. But then it hit me that the courts have appointed an attorney for me. It could also be the shitty ass D.A. too. I heard D.A,'s pop up on inmates all the time, trying to get them to cop to a plea deal. But I'm not taking this lying down. I've been locked up for three days now so I'm gonna fight this thing to the end. It doesn't matter if Julian turned his back on me. I'm a fighter and I refuse to let the prosecutor hit me in the head with a ten to a twenty-year prison sentence. No way!

While contemplating on what to say to the D.A or court-appointed attorney, I heard a male's voice say, "She's in that second booth." And then I heard, woman say, "Thank you."

“Yes, thank you,” a male said, giving me a hint that I was getting a visit from both a man and a woman. But who? Was it Tammy coming down here to rub shit in my face?

With my heart beating uncontrollably, I closed my eyes, took a deep breath and then I exhaled. The moment I opened my eyes a black woman with a layered bob hair cut appeared on the other side of the glass, carrying an expensive briefcase. She was an average looking woman, but she was dressed to the nine in a Gucci pants suit. She was the type of woman that would command attention when he walks into a room. But when the man with her appeared before me, I almost lost it. My heart nearly jumped out of my chest because I was so overwhelmed with emotions. "Happy to see me?" Julian asked.

I nodded and I said, yes simultaneously.

“This is Natalie Norvelle. She’s your attorney and we’re gonna get you out of here.” He said confidently.

“But my bail is so high.” I pointed out.

"Don't worry about that, I gotcha' covered."

“Really?!” I said, getting filled with tears.

“Yes, baby. You’re coming home. And we’re gonna fight this to the end.” He insisted.

After hearing Julian's words, I couldn't hold back the tears any longer. He was really here to bring me home. But, what's gonna happen when he finds out that I had something to do with those murders? Will he still stick by me? I guess I'll have to wait and see.

SNEAK PEAK INTO "BEHIND CLOSED DOOR"

(Book in Stores Now)

CHAPTER ONE

My Screwed Up Life

The sun sparkled over the Epstein family's summer home in the Hamptons. The sunlit lawn is why they'd chosen the property. The home was a huge mansion in an exclusive gated community, sat on top of a hill with gorgeous views from every room. The natural sunlight hit the well-manicured lawn like a movie spotlight. Evelyn Epstein stood with her arms folded across her chest, staring out at the massive landscape. She inhaled the fresh scent of the newly cut grass and let out a long-exasperated breath. She had so much on her mind. Evelyn and her family had been coming to the Hamptons from New York City each summer for eighteen years now, and with every passing year, the façade they put on of the perfect little family seemed to crack a little more. She shuddered just thinking about how much things had crumbled. No more picture-perfect life for Evelyn a thought that made her want to cry.

This summer was the worst it had ever been. Evelyn had walked hand and hand with her husband Levi into the high-class house parties of the Hampton's elite, although her marriage was all but over. It had been at her urging that they acted as if things were still wonderful at home. Evelyn had also smiled, chuckled and told several people that her daughter was away in Europe studying anthropology, although her only child was tucked away from the probing eyes in drug rehab four hours away from the Hamptons. The best lie of all, however; was how Evelyn had played the role of a happy-go-lucky, faithful wife, although she had been plotting for months on how to get even with her husband by finding her own love affair. Evelyn had to admit, this time she felt more powerful than she ever had during her entire marriage. Yes, it was a crazy time at the Epstein home.

Evelyn didn't know how much more of a horse and pony show she could put on for all of her superficial, "happily married" friends. She was dying slowly inside. The fake smiles and all of the lies were wearing on her. She had literally watched her perfect life fade into obscurity. She was in a loveless marriage; her only child was a drug addict; and, now she had found out how her husband had been keeping them afloat financially all of these years since his family had shut him out of his late father's wealth. Things were spiraling downward fast. Evelyn had always thought of herself as being in full control of it all. Not now. The reality of just how little control she had was never more evident than now.

Evelyn closed her eyes when she heard Levi approaching from behind. She smelled his signature, Ralph Lauren Safari cologne before he even made it to where she stood. She flinched as Levi placed one hand on her shoulder and pecked her on her cheek. More like a brother would perfunctorily kiss his sister. "How are you?" he asked dryly. Evelyn cracked a halfhearted smile, her back going rigid and her shoulders stiffening under his touch. It was all she could do to keep her composure, to keep from punching, slapping, and spitting on him. She couldn't find one ounce of love left for her husband. Their once undying love had withered into contempt, resentments, and regrets. She was sure Levi could tell from her body language that she wasn't up for any small talk from him.

"You're up early," Levi commented, flashing a perfectly veneered fake smile. Levi wasn't going to let Evelyn kill his refreshed spirit with her normal sour mood. He never looked Evelyn in the eyes anymore. She knew it was because of his guilt for his latest conquest. "I guess you have your day planned already…" he continued the small talk with no response from Evelyn. He set something down next to him and by Evelyn's side. That got her attention right away. She looked down and peered at Levi's suitcase. She rolled her eyes and bit into her bottom lip. She could feel the heat rising from her chest, and her hands involuntarily curled into fists. Levi noticed his wife's body language. He wore an expression that said not again. The manufactured drama was getting old fast.

"I won't be gone long. I promise. I'll be back in time for Diane's annual all-white affair. I know how much that means to you," Levi explained, dryly garnering no response in his wife's body language. He knew that keeping up appearances for her friends was more important to Evelyn than anything he could ever do to make her happy again. Evelyn turned towards Levi abruptly, causing him to take a step back. She moved in like a lion towards its prey, her eyes in evil slits.

"Did you forget your daughter is graduating from the rehabilitation center today?" Evelyn asked, her voice low, almost a growl. She eyed him evilly, her nostrils moving in and out. She had one shaky finger jutted accusingly towards Levi, and her other hand balled so tightly her nails dug moon-shaped craters into her palms. She was tired of playing second fiddle in Levi's life. But, if he was going to treat her like she didn't exist…fine, but now their only child.

"I didn't forget. I told you I have a very important business meeting," he replied, annoyed. "I left her a gift on the table inside. There's a note there and a little something to make up for my absence," Levi finished flatly without looking his wife in the eyes. He immediately signaled for his driver to grab his bags. In his assessment, there was nothing else to talk about. Levi knew how their confrontations would end up. He had long since grown tired of Evelyn's constant guilt trips and self-pity parties. She had definitely become a shell of her former vibrant, outgoing, attention-commanding self. She was far from the woman he'd married.

"So that's it? You throw money at her again? A goddamn note Levi?! Is that all you can offer her?! You think a note can make up for your absence?!" Are we back to our same antics again? Your family comes second to the new whore!" Evelyn barked at her husband's back. "It was your money that got her where she is in the first place!" Levi gave her a look that sent a chill down her spine before he continued on.

"Levi! I am talking to you!" Evelyn called out again. He ignored her and rushed down the front steps. Before she could say another word, Levi climbed into the back of his Mercedes May Bach and slammed the door. Evelyn rocked on her heels as she watched the car ease down the long pathway towards the road. That was it. Just like that, Levi was gone again.

Evelyn had been through the same thing so many times she had come to expect it. She had recognized all the signs that Levi was having yet another affair. It had been a month since she'd gotten the photographs from the private investigator that had confirmed her suspicions. This time Levi had crossed the line; he'd gotten disrespectful and disgusting with his philandering.

When Evelyn had reviewed the photos of Levi and his new mistress, she'd thrown up the entire contents of her stomach. The same gut sickening feeling had come over her again, but this time was different…more personal.

Evelyn could feel her heart throbbing against her chest bone now just thinking about it. She guessed this was what a broken heart felt like. It wasn't a new feeling, and she didn't know why it always felt like a fresh wound. Evelyn silently chastised herself for being so emotional all of the time. It had been twenty-two years since she'd met and married who she thought was the man of her dreams and he'd been unfaithful at least ten or more of those years. She closed her eyes to stifle the angry tears threatening to fall. Instead, she headed into the house to make a phone call. "Two can play the game this time around Levi Epstein," she mumbled as she stormed through the house. There would be no more victim roll for Evelyn. No. She planned to be victorious this time around.

Evelyn had just stepped off the runway at New York's Fashion week when she'd first met Levi in 1989. Evelyn's perfect ivory skin went flush with red when Levi approached her at the after-show reception. Everyone who was anyone in New York City knew who Levi Epstein was—the gorgeous and very wealthy son of Ari Epstein, New York's most wealthy real estate tycoon. It was a well-known fact that Levi Epstein could have any woman in the world he wanted. Not only was he strikingly attractive, he was rich and single, and the opportunities that came his way were abundant. He was thirty-five and number one on the most eligible bachelor list; a fact that was not lost on Evelyn when Levi approached her flashing his perfect smile and displaying the charm of a storybook prince. He immediately grabbed her hand and planted his perfect lips on the top of it. It was something like electricity that had coursed through Evelyn's body, but she had done a fabulous job of keeping her composure.

Standing together, they looked like the perfect Hollywood couple. Evelyn's statuesque six-foot frame was adorned with a beautiful, teal, Donna Karan dress that dipped low in the back exposing her firm, muscular frame. The dress had fit her svelte body like it had been sewn on. Perfectly coifed, dark brown, ringlets of hair danced around her face and picked up the chestnut in her eyes.

"You were stunning in the show," Levi had said to her. His smile was a lady-killer. Evelyn had felt a whoosh of breath leave her lungs in response to his smooth baritone. Although she looked like a grown woman, Evelyn was only nineteen years old and hadn't had much time to date. Levi's beautiful grey eyes and his neatly trimmed jet-black hair had overwhelmed her. He reminded Evelyn of a younger Brad Pitt. Looking at him made her pulse quicken, so she lowered her eyes, stared down into her drink, and smiled girlishly.

"You probably say that to all of the models," Evelyn murmured, still averting direct eye contact. Levi had placed his finger under her chin and urged her to look at him. Evelyn reluctantly locked eyes with him, and when he smiled, she swore she could feel her heart-melting. Standing in his presence, Evelyn felt like they were the only two people in the large, crowded ballroom. They'd spent the entire reception laughing and talking about everything from runway fashions to politics. Levi had asked Evelyn if he could call her sometime and maybe take her out. She'd told him that she was leaving for Milan the next day and would be gone for two months. Levi had told her that was all the more reason he wanted to get to know her—she was a woman with her own life. He'd asked if she would leave her contact information so that he could call her sometime. She scribbled her information down on a silver trimmed napkin. Levi pushed it into his lapel pocket. "Right next to my heart," he'd said, tapping the place where he had put her number. That made Evelyn blush all over again. She was smitten.

After her third day in Milan, Evelyn returned to her hotel one night to find the entire room filled with beautiful long stem pink, red, and white roses. She was flabbergasted when she'd read the card, "You are as pretty as a newly blossomed rose. I came to Milan just to see you. Please call. Levi Epstein."

Evelyn had flopped down on her bed, weak with joy. The other two lanky beauties she had been rooming with snickered and made love faces and googly eyes at her. "Call him! Call him," They had twirled around her, urging her to call Levi right away, but Evelyn opted to wait until the next day. She didn't want him to think she was that easy to win over. When she'd finally called, Levi officially asked her out on a date. They went on their first date, and it had been magical—a gondola ride, dinner at a quaint Italian eatery, and a romantic walk through the city at night. Evelyn was overwhelmed with feelings she'd never experienced in her life. It had to be love.

Levi had wanted to know all about her life. He'd been the first man to ever care about the little things that mattered to her, like her childhood and how she'd become a high fashion model at such a young age. They spent another night talking into the wee hours of the morning. It was like they had been made for each other from the start. Evelyn had never experienced anything like what she had that night. No one had ever shown her the kind of interest that Levi had shown her. Levi felt the same as well. He had always had women swooning over him, but none had ever held his interest as long as Evelyn had. It was like a fateful love that was meant to be from the start.

Levi stayed in Milan for a week wining and dining Evelyn after her fashion photoshoots and shows. He wanted to make sure that she knew that he wanted her; that he was interested in her; and that, he intended on making this a regular occurrence. He'd showered her with beautiful premier designer gifts. Levi had spared no expense. He felt like it was the least he could do for this beauty he had found. Before he left Milan, Levi asked Evelyn to call him when she returned to New York. She had initially acted as if she had had to "think about it," but Evelyn knew the real truth about how she was feeling inside. She could hardly sit still for her entire flight from Milan to New York City. Evelyn had called as soon as her plane landed at JFK Airport. Her hands had trembled as she had dialed his number from a cold payphone right inside of the airport. Evelyn was relieved when he'd answered. She literally melted inside once she was able to speak to the man; she knew she was falling in love with. Levi was all she could think of for the time she remained in Milan without him. She had crazy feelings of longing. So much so that the other girls had teased her incessantly until their job in Milan was done.

Evelyn and Levi met the day after her return to New York, and they had officially begun dating. Levi had given her a single flower he'd picked from Central Park and said, "would you be mine?" They had shared a hearty laugh at Levi's antics, but Evelyn had surely accepted the little wilting flower and his invitation to date him.

Levi made Evelyn feel like she was the only woman in the world every single day. There was never a dull moment with him. Not only did he shower her with gifts, but he'd taken her to all of New York's most exclusive invite-only social events and acted as if he was so proud to have her on his arm. Levi was such a gentleman. He was extremely, loving, and he paid attention to every detail of their relationship. People always commented on what a beautiful couple they made. After a year of dating, Levi finally proposed. When he'd presented Evelyn with his great grandmother's sapphire and diamond engagement ring, Evelyn almost wet herself. She jumped into his arms screaming, "yes! yes! yes!" Levi's parents weren't happy with his choice. They would have preferred a good, clean, Jewish girl for their youngest son. Evelyn had grown up Catholic. She was certainly no virgin if she was a model; Levi's mother had complained. Evelyn also didn't have parents, which alarmed the Epsteins. "What is a girl without a mother?! No mother, no religion, what else Levi!" Levi's mother had screamed in her usual theatrical performance manner. Levi had heard his mother's "dream girl" for him so many times that he went out and found the complete opposite.

Evelyn so head over heels in love quickly agreed to go through the process of converting to

Judaism. Levi's parents; defeated by Evelyn and Levi's love; finally settled. Evelyn and Levi were married in a traditional Jewish ceremony. The wedding took place on a white sand beach adjacent to Ari Epstein's $40 million-dollar estate in the Caribbean island of Turks and Caicos. Four hundred guests attended the lavish wedding; of which, only twenty-five were Evelyn's friends—people she'd befriended while modeling. The remainder of the guests she'd never even met. At the time, Evelyn didn't dare complain. She felt like she was living a dream; far from what she could have ever envisioned for herself. As an orphan who'd grown up poor, Evelyn never dreamed she'd become a world-renowned model, but more importantly, that she'd be married to one of the most coveted men in the United States. On all accounts, Evelyn thought she'd walked into heaven. It didn't take long for her to realize she'd been sadly mistaken. Life with Levi had changed so drastically, sometimes Evelyn couldn't believe he was the same man she'd met back then.

"Mrs. Epstein your car is out front," Carolynn announced snapping Evelyn out of her reverie. Evelyn hadn't even realized she'd been staring into space. She quickly dabbed at her eyes and turned towards Carolynn. Carolynn smiled at her, realizing she had interrupted Evelyn's thoughts.

"I want everything to be perfect for Arianna when she gets here. Please make sure the caterers are on time and the tent…the decorations have to be perfect. Her favorite color is blue. The cake is supposed to be delivered in two hours. The guests should arrive…I just…" Evelyn rambled; an edge of nerves apparent in her words. Carolynn put her hand up and let a warm smile spread across her face. She knew her boss was nervous.

"Mrs. E, I will have everything in order. I know how important this day is to you and to Ari," Carolynn comforted, her warm smile easing the tension in the air. Evelyn exhaled and thanked Carolynn. She trusted Carolynn who'd worked for the family since Arianna was born. Only, Evelyn, Levi, and Carolynn knew the truth about the purpose of the big party. Carolynn knew all of the family's secrets. She had become a part of their family; thus, she knew every detail of their lives. She followed Evelyn around the huge master suite making sure Evelyn didn't forget anything. Carolynn gave the room a once over. Everything seemed to be all right.

Evelyn grabbed her Hermes Birkin and looked at herself one last time in the long Victorian-style mirror that took up almost an entire wall in the master suite. She was still a knockout, even at forty-one years old. Admittedly, she had a little help from one of the top plastic surgeons in New York, a nip here and a tuck there, but her natural beauty still came through. Her face showed only a few crow's feet at the corners of her eyes, nothing a little Restylane couldn't cure she thought. She'd just gotten rid of her laugh lines a week prior, and she'd gotten her lips filled in while she was at it. Evelyn had opted to use collagen fillers instead of Botox-like most of her friends. Carolynn smiled as she watched her boss go over her outfit again and again. It was a habit Evelyn hadn't broken in all these years. Carolynn knew Evelyn's next move before she even did it. Just as anticipated, Evelyn ran her hands over the flat part of her stomach and turned sideways to make sure her Spanx were doing their job. It was flat as a board. Perfect.

She wore a pair of white, wide-legged crepe Versace sailor pants that complimented her long, still model-like slim legs. Carolyn assisted Evelyn as she shrugged into a short, navy Diane Von Furstenberg blazer to complete her look. Evelyn adjusted her newly lifted D cup breasts and examined her neck and jaw lines to make sure her tanning bed hadn't left any streaks. She smiled at herself and then back at Carolynn.

"Not so bad for the mother of an eighteen-year-old, huh Carolynn?" Evelyn posed the question she really didn't want the answer to.

"Beautiful," Carolynn praised on queue. They'd had this same routine for the longest.

Evelyn chuckled. She knew she was the quintessential kept woman. Through it all, she had managed to keep herself in tiptop shape, and with the assistance of her plastic surgeon, she still got mistaken for a woman in her thirties. As she headed out of the house towards her waiting ride, her cell phone buzzed in her bag. Evelyn fished around and retrieved it. Instinctively a smile spread across her face. “Hello lover,” she cooed into the mobile device as she slid into the back of the Bentley that awaited her. Evelyn closed her eyes; maybe the day wouldn’t be as bad as she’d thought it would be. Especially if she could slip away after she did her motherly duty.

CHAPTER TWO

Family First

People rushed around her, but that didn't distract Evelyn at all. She kept her head up high as she sat on one of the hard-wooden seats inside the auditorium of the Passages Rehabilitation Center. Her palms were sweaty, and she couldn't keep her legs from rocking back and forth. Evelyn was clearly out of her element, but she knew she had to be there regardless. She kept telling herself, "it is my duty."

Evelyn looked around at some of the parents there, just like her, most seemed to be well off. Evelyn tried not to stare too long, but she couldn't help it. She felt a pang of jealousy looking at some of the couples holding hands and being supportive of each other. Seemingly happy families made her stomach churn. She wished that were her life again. Damn you, Levi.

Evelyn shook her head to clear it and tried to focus on why she was there—for her child. Her only child. And it had cost them $100,000 to get Arianna the treatment she needed. It was an expense neither Evelyn nor Levi could argue wasn't necessary. Private drug rehabilitation was expensive, but in Evelyn's assessment, there was no amount of money that could keep her from trying to save her daughter or save face with her friends was more like it. There was no way Evelyn could stand for any of her socialite friends to find out Arianna was addicted to drugs and had been living like a virtual vagabond. The thought of anyone finding out made a cold chill shoot down Evelyn's spine. She hunched her shoulders in an attempt to relax, but the thoughts still hovered.

Evelyn remembered clearly how devastated she was when she found out their princess was addicted to methamphetamine. It was Carolynn who'd nervously told Evelyn about Arianna's addiction. Evelyn also thought back to how Levi had screamed at her and told her it was all her fault that his daughter was an embarrassment to the Epstein name. He had told Evelyn it was Evelyn's "trashy" DNA and family lineage that had caused their daughter to be such a disappointment. It hadn't been the first time Levi had used Evelyn's upbringing against her during an argument.

"Mother," Evelyn heard the familiar voice from behind her. She popped up out of her seat and cleared away the thoughts that had been crowding her mind. Evelyn took in an eyeful of her only child. She tilted her head and clasped her hand over her mouth. Tears welled up in her eyes immediately when she went to grab for her daughter.

"Oh, sweetheart...you look amazing. This time away has done wonders. I am so proud of you," Evelyn cried, grabbing her daughter in a tight embrace. Evelyn felt a warm feeling of relief wash over her. Arianna finally presented like something Evelyn could be proud of. Evelyn squeezed Arianna again. "Thank God," she whispered. Evelyn was really thanking God for bringing her daughter back from the brink of death. What would her friends have thought if Arianna had gave way to a drug addiction? Evelyn would've suffered the worst embarrassment of her life. Evelyn shook off those worse case scenarios and tried to relish in the moment.

It was a miracle that Arianna was even alive. The night Evelyn and Levi had signed Arianna into the rehabilitation center involuntarily, Arianna had looked like death warmed over. Her skin had been ghostly pale, and dark rings rimmed the bottoms of her eyes. Arianna's dark hair had been matted in clumps around her scalp, and her body was gaunt, almost skeletal. She smelled like she hadn't had a bath in weeks and her clothes, although expensive, were filthy. Arianna had been out on a binge for three weeks while Evelyn and Levi worried sick and had people out scouring the entire city for her. It had been the first time they'd come together for anything in years. Levi had even hugged Evelyn a few of the nights they'd both sat up worrying about their daughter. Arianna had kicked and screamed when she'd first arrived at the center. She cursed at her parents and told her mother she hated her. She'd screamed and begged Levi not to let Evelyn sign her into the center. Arianna blamed Evelyn for everything. Evelyn was an emotional wreck that night. She also blamed herself for it all, although she knew it wasn't entirely her fault. Levi had remained cool as a cucumber, as usual. "Daddy loves you. Daddy loves you," Levi had repeated to his daughter over and over again. He never once defended Evelyn and told his daughter she needed the help. It was something Evelyn filed in her mental Rolodex. The hurt she'd felt was almost tangible.

All of that was the past Evelyn told herself now. Just like all of the other hurts she'd suffered at the hands of her daughter and husband, Evelyn swallowed them like hard marbles. Seeing Arianna now—cheeks rosy, body filled out in all of the right places, hair shiny and straight, made Evelyn warm inside. Arianna had taken the best of Evelyn and Levi's features. She stood almost six feet tall and was built like a runway model. She had long slender legs, a small waist, and small breasts. Arianna had exquisite, thick, jet-black hair and slate grey eyes. She had inherited Evelyn's high cheekbones and perfect nose, and with Levi's prominent chin, her face was striking. From the time she was a small child, Arianna had turned heads everywhere she went. She was more of a showstopper than both of her parents to say the least.

Evelyn finally relinquished her grasp on Arianna and gave her a good once over. Evelyn smiled wide; she thought her daughter looked perfect. Arianna was dressed conservatively in a maroon Donna Karan sheath dress that Carolynn had picked out; a pair of kitten-heeled Jimmy Choo's and a simple cardigan to top off her look. Arianna finally looked like an eighteen-year-old wealthy J.A.P (Jewish American Princess) should. Evelyn was satisfied, but she still couldn't say she was ever proud to say that Arianna was her daughter. It had always been a struggle being a mother to Arianna. Evelyn squeezed Arianna and grabbed for Arianna's hand, hoping to get a return show of affection. But Arianna impolitely let her arms hang limp at her side. Evelyn knew right away that her daughter was in rare form. It was the norm for Arianna to treat Evelyn like she had no regard for her at all.

"Where's dad?" Arianna asked petulantly. Evelyn released her daughter's hand quickly. She looked at Arianna seriously. She wanted to scream in Arianna's face and say I am here for you! Isn't that enough! He was never there for you like I have been! But Evelyn kept her thoughts to herself; kept smiling and kept doing what she did best—pretending.

"Oh, Ari darling, this is your day. Don't worry about the small things. You look so good…so healthy now," Evelyn replied sympathetically. She cracked a phony smile and hugged her daughter again, hoping they could move off the subject of Levi. "You are simply stunning Ari, I can't say that enough," Evelyn followed up, flashing her plastic smile again. Nothing seemed to faze Arianna.

"I guess you would say I look good now since you haven't seen me in six months. All you have to compare it to is the way I looked when you forced me into this hell hole," Arianna replied sharply, as she squirmed out of her mother's stifling embrace. Evelyn felt like someone had slapped her across the face. She inhaled. It was taking all she had to keep it together now.

Evelyn ignored the comment. She already felt awful enough about not visiting, but she'd figured that Arianna needed time away without the influence of her parents. Evelyn had been afraid that if she'd visited, Arianna would ask her questions about her father. Evelyn had always tried to shelter Arianna from the reality that her father was a philandering whore. Evelyn's sugar-coating Levi's indiscretions only made Arianna see Evelyn as the bad guy and Levi as the hero in their lives. The past six months had been no different. Levi cheated, and Evelyn covered up. She hid his ways from Arianna; their friends; his parents…everyone. It became like a fulltime job for Evelyn. Faking, like her life, was still picture perfect. This time was slightly different. Now as Arianna shot accusing eyes at her, Evelyn guiltily thought about her own preoccupation while her daughter was gone and wanted to veer away from the topic of why she didn't visit.

"So are you ready to go home? You must be excited to get back to life. There are so many good things waiting for you. Whatever you want, you can have," Evelyn asked, changing the subject while fidgeting with her newly purchased monstrous twelve-carat canary diamond ring. It was one of many things she'd purchased on spite after finding out the identity of Levi's most recent mistress.

"Yeah going home…I can hardly wait to get back to that life. I'll see you after the ceremony," Arianna droned gruffly, stomping away from her mother. Evelyn looked around to see if anyone had noticed the strained interaction between them. She smiled weakly at a couple that had been watching. Evelyn's cheeks flamed over when she noticed them. She wondered how much of the conversation they had overheard. "These children. We have to love them," Evelyn chortled, averting her eyes away from the gawking pair. She turned her face away and dabbed at the tears threatening to drop from her eyes. Even her baby girl hated her. Evelyn couldn't win for trying. Nothing was ever good enough for Arianna and Levi. Years later, she still couldn't please them.

The night Arianna was born Levi had missed the entire birth—from labor to the minute Arianna took her first breath. Evelyn had spent sixteen hours in labor at Lenox Hill Hospital, and Levi never showed up for a minute of it. Both of Levi's parents had come rushing into Evelyn's private birthing room in a huff when they'd gotten the news that their newest member was about to arrive. But neither of them could explain why their son hadn't been around when Evelyn tried to reach him. Levi's parents had long since stopped making excuses for Levi because they knew Evelyn wasn't buying it anymore. Evelyn felt that their presence at the birth was only because they secretly hoped she would provide them with a grandson to carry on the Epstein name. Evelyn had known for months she was carrying a baby girl, but she never told Levi or his parents. She knew how Jews really felt about having first-born girls. She also knew they only tolerated her as it was. Evelyn hadn't felt that alone in a room full of people since her days living in an orphanage. Nurses, Levi's parents, doctors, all circled around her, providing for her every need. But no one could soothe the ache of loneliness she felt for Levi.

After a horrendous labor, Evelyn had given birth to a perfect little girl through cesarean section. She'd made sure she got her tummy tucked at the same time. She wouldn't have wanted to disappoint Levi by not keeping herself up. Evelyn had already suspected that Levi was stepping out with other women behind her back.

The baby girl was a perfect, pink-faced, screaming bundle of joy. She had Levi's grey eyes and prominent chin, with Evelyn's long limbs and button nose. "Let's call her Ari…after her grandfather," Levi's mother had said after she laid eyes on her granddaughter. Ari Epstein, Levi's father agreed and who was Evelyn to argue with such a powerful patriarch. Whatever the Epsteins wanted, the Epsteins got. Evelyn had learned that the hard way. The naming of her first child would be no different.

Evelyn, too physically and mentally exhausted to protest, compromised with the Epstein's and they all agreed to call the baby, Arianna Bethany Epstein. Or baby Ari for short. Evelyn thought it was a fair compromise given the fact that she had always wanted to name her first daughter Beth Ann, after a mother she had never known. She never told the Epsteins of her desires; instead, she came up with a name she thought she could live with.

When Levi finally showed up at the hospital to see his new baby, he smelled of a woman's perfume and looked like he'd been partying for days. He leaned in to give Evelyn an obligatory kiss, and she had turned her face away. It was all she could do to keep from making a scene in front of Levi's parents and to hide the hot tears that were threatening to spring from her eyes. Evelyn had tried to hold onto her anger and bitterness that first night Levi came to her bedside, but, after witnessing Levi hold his daughter with such care and sensitivity and watching him seemingly fall in love with his daughter, Evelyn had been overwhelmed with that old, gushy, head-over-heels feeling for Levi once again. It was like when they were in Milan, falling in love all over again. Evelyn had told herself that night in the hospital that for her child and the sake of her family, she would do anything it took to make them happy. It was a promise she would come to suffer to keep.

Things were great for a while after Arianna's birth. Evelyn felt like she'd finally gotten her husband back. In the beginning, Levi was a doting father and a caring husband. He showered Evelyn with gift after expensive gift. He'd told her the gifts were to thank her for giving him his greatest gift of all. He spent hours holding baby Ari, talking, and singing to her. So much so, Evelyn had shamefully grown a little jealous of how much attention Levi showered on the baby. But once again, Evelyn put her feelings aside and tried to make the best of the situation. Evelyn saw herself as just mother and wife. There was no more individual Evelyn. The things she wanted, needed and liked came secondary in her life. Evelyn spent every waking minute pleasing her daughter and her husband. She'd lost herself in meeting the needs of Levi and Arianna. But it was with the help of the hired hands of course. At some point, Evelyn grew to resent her life. Each day, she would perfunctorily put on a happy face.

As Arianna grew older, Evelyn and Levi gave her anything she asked for…materially anyway.

From birth, Arianna was a trust fund baby. She was worth more than some celebrities five times her age, and she hadn't even turned a year old. Papa Epstein, which is what Levi's father asked to be called, had made sure his granddaughter would never have to lift a finger in her life. Evelyn felt a sense of security knowing that unlike herself as a child, her daughter would never want for anything.

There were extravagant nurseries built for baby Ari in every home Levi owned, even in his two New York City penthouses. Arianna was royalty in the eyes of the entire Epstein family. She had been given dance lessons from the age of two. She had a private acting coach as soon as she turned five. Papa Ari purchased a thoroughbred riding horse for Arianna's tenth birthday and equestrian lessons to match. She'd had huge, extravagant birthday parties every year with a guest list of A-list celebrity children. For her Bat Mitzvah, they'd flown in dresses from Paris, Milan, and London. Once a year Evelyn and Levi would take Arianna on vacation to parts of the world she couldn't even pronounce. Private schools were the only kind ever considered for Arianna. She'd been provided an allowance of $1,000 per week from the time she was thirteen years old. Even after the huge Bat Mitzvah, Arianna's sweet sixteen was thrown on a yacht and cost more than some celebrity weddings. But, as she got older, Arianna realized that nothing her parents gave her could replace spending time with them every day or having at least one sit down dinner with them like she'd seen done in families on television. Carolynn was the person who showed up for school meetings, plays, and trips. Levi and Evelyn hardly knew anything concrete about their daughter's wants and needs. Evelyn was too busy keeping tabs on Levi to notice.

After a while, nothing Levi and Evelyn gave Arianna seemed like enough. They poured money into any activity she picked up—gymnastics, soccer, synchronized swimming, lacrosse, equestrian, golf, polo, and, tennis. Arianna would grow bored and quit. She had grown to be spoiled and angry. By the time she was seventeen, Arianna was deep into the New York party and drug scene. She fashioned herself as one of New York City's brat pack socialites. Late night party scenes became her daily life. She'd grown up and become best friends with former child stars, daughters of hotel magnates and children of rock stars. Unflattering paparazzi pictures of Arianna had shown up at least two dozen times in People and Us magazines. When confronted, Arianna would scream and throw tantrums. Evelyn had admittedly dropped the ball when it came to paying her daughter the attention she was craving. But she blamed Levi for it all, and he blamed her just the same.

Evelyn and Arianna's ride from the rehabilitation center was tensely silent. It was as if a joyous occasion had not just happened. Arianna was brooding the entire ride, and Evelyn was trying to please as usual. The pomp and circumstance of Arianna's rehab graduation faded quicker than an eclipse of the sun. Afterward, Evelyn had tried to make small talk, about the weather, Arianna's clothes, her new cell phone. When that didn't work, Evelyn tried to tell Arianna how proud she was of her accomplishments—getting clean and sober in six months. Evelyn had told Arianna that she imagined it hadn't been easy. Arianna ignored her mother, for the most part, dropping a vicious insult in response here and there. It wasn't lost on either of them how many times Evelyn's cell phone had buzzed and interrupted their tense exchange. Arianna had even raised an eyebrow to her mother and said, "Why don't you stop pretending to be interested in speaking to me and just answer your phone?" Evelyn's cheeks had flamed over at her daughter's comment. "No one is more important that you Ari," Evelyn had replied. It didn't make a difference. She was clearly not going to make Arianna happy.

Finally, too exasperated to continue practically begging her daughter to talk to her, Evelyn gave up. Arianna rudely put her iPod earphones in and turned the volume up so loud Evelyn could hear every curse word in the lyrics of the rock music she listened to. Arianna also took to texting incessantly on her cell phone, one of the luxuries she had missed while locked up in that place. Defeated, Evelyn resorted to watching the passing scenery outside of the Bentley's darkly tinted windows. Evelyn secretly wished she were someplace else. She could think of a million things she would've rather be doing than taking her daughter's verbal abuse. Evelyn's mind drifted to things she found pleasurable. Of course, she thought about Max, her new friend. The thoughts seemed to ease the pain of the long ride. Evelyn found herself growing a little flush with some of the thoughts Max conjured in her mind.

When the car pulled up to the gate leading up to the house, Arianna yanked her earphones out of her ears and bolted upright in her seat. "I'm not going to the summer house, I'm going to the city…the penthouse," she announced brusquely. Evelyn's eyebrows shot up, and her pulse sped up. Arianna had been practically living alone at their Upper East Side penthouse when she'd disappeared and ultimately gotten herself in trouble. Evelyn didn't think it was a good idea for her to go back into that environment so soon. Evelyn wanted Carolynn to keep an eye on Arianna. Of course, Evelyn didn't have time herself for babysitting a teenager right now. That's what they'd paid Carolynn to do all of these years.

"Ari, please," Evelyn said as calmly as she could given the circumstances. "You need to be around us…your loved ones. We all missed you so much. Carolynn is looking forward to seeing you. I want to catch up. You can go to the penthouse another day," Evelyn tried to reason, touching her daughter's leg gently. Arianna tilted her head and looked at her mother through squinted eyes. The look sent a chill down Evelyn's back.

"Please mother. Don't start this bullshit. Concerned mother doesn't fit you well. You don't want to catch up or spend quality time with me…you never have and never will," Arianna hissed, pushing Evelyn's hand off of her knee roughly. Evelyn snatched her hand back as if a venomous snake had bitten her. She pinched the bridge of her nose, trying to quell the throbbing that had suddenly started between her eyes. It was starting again, already—the hate/hate relationship she had with her only child. Evelyn often blamed herself for not bonding with Arianna as a baby. She let out a long breath that seemed to zap all of her energy. Everything seemed to stand still.

"I don't want to be here if my father is not here. I'm over the Hamptons and all of your fake friends. I'm sure you have some kind of party planned for me in there, but I'm not coming. I refuse to be like you mother…a fucking fake, hiding behind money, Botox, and designer clothes… living a big lie. Now either you let me go where I want to go, or you get even more embarrassed when I go in there and tell everyone what a wonderful time, I had in drug rehab,"

Arianna spat viciously. Evelyn coughed or more like gagged. She felt like her daughter had gut-punched her. She placed her hand on her chest, shocked by her daughter's outburst. She looked over at her only child, and she swore she could see red flames flickering in Arianna's eyes. Pure hatred clouded the girls face. Evelyn's jaw rocked feverishly, and her pulse pounded. Suddenly everything was swirling around her. She cleared her throat like she'd done so many times when preparing to speak to Levi, thinking, Arianna had grown to be just like her father. Evelyn knew she couldn't let Arianna ruin what she had spent years building—the lie that was their life.

"Arianna, I have tried and tried. What more do you want me to do? It is not my fault that your father is not here. I asked him to be here, and he chose to attend a business meeting..." Evelyn started, steeling herself for more cruelty from Arianna. Arianna's face lit blood red, her eyebrows folded into a scowl.

"No! Shut up!" Arianna screamed. "You probably ran him off like you always do. I don't know how he stayed married to you after all of these years with all of your nagging and complaining. Matter of fact, I do know. He stayed with you because of me! It's my fault that my poor father has to endure life with a bitch like you!" Arianna continued with her vituperative tirade. She yanked on the door handle, as the car had started moving through the open gate up the pathway to the house. The driver slammed on the breaks in response. Evelyn's body jerked forward then back, and her head slammed into the headrest. Her heart began pounding even harder, and her head throbbed.

"Oh, my God! Arianna!" Evelyn screamed, wincing, and holding the back of her head. The car had screeched to a halt, and Arianna scrambled out of the door. There was nothing Evelyn could do now.

"Ari! Wait!" Evelyn hung her head out of the door and screamed. It was too late. Visibly shaken, Evelyn decided against running after her daughter. There was, but so much she could take. She knew that Arianna was serious when she said she would tell everyone she was not in Europe; but in a rehab. Someplace deep inside, what all of her friends thought was more important than forcing her daughter to enjoy the lavish party she had prepared.

"Everything alright, Mrs. E?" their driver asked. Evelyn was terribly embarrassed and equally as flustered. "You want me to go after her?" he asked, peering at Evelyn through the rearview mirror.

"I'm fine. She's a teenager," Evelyn replied, trying to seem lighthearted about the incident, but not able to control her voice shaking. "Take me up to the house and come back for her. Take her wherever she wants to go. If she wants to go to the city, let her go to the city," Evelyn croaked out instructions to the driver, her voice finally shedding the false cheeriness she tried on; instead, her words came out laced with pain and anger. It was better than Arianna blowing the whistle on Evelyn's lies.

Once in front of the house, Evelyn climbed from the car. She steeled herself for the questions and shocked looks she knew she'd face when she stepped inside of her home. Evelyn immediately began constructing more lies in her head. She had become so good at it now that it took her no time to think of what she'd tell her friends about Arianna's whereabouts. Evelyn exhaled a windstorm before she turned the doorknob to her home. It was the first time she had acknowledged that she was losing the battle on all fronts, but she'd made it up in her mind that it wouldn't be for long.

THE END OF PREVIEW-
IN STORES NOW...

Sneak Peak into "Cheaper to Keep Her part 1"

(Book in Stores Now)

Prologue

"Bitch! You better open this fucking door!"

When I heard his voice, the banging and then the kicking on the door, my heart sank into the pit of my stomach. A hot flash came over my body at the sound of his deep, baritone voice. I could tell he was more than livid. I immediately started rushing through the luxury high-rise condominium I had been living in for the past six months. Duke owned it. It was time to put my Plan B into motion. Quick, fast and in a hurry.

"Damn, damn, shit!" I cursed as I gathered shit up. I didn't know how I had let myself get caught slipping. I planned to be the fuck out of dodge before Duke could get wind of my bad deeds. I had definitely not planned my escape correctly.

"Lynise!" Duke's voice boomed again with additional angry urgency. He started banging even harder and jiggling the doorknob. I was scared to death, but I wasn't shocked. I knew sooner or later he would come. After all the shit I had done to him, I would've come after my ass too.

"Lynise! Open this fucking door now!" Duke continued to bark from the other side of the door. He didn't sound like the man I had met and fell in love with. He damn sure didn't sound like he was about to shower me with cash and gifts like he used to. Not after all the shit, I had done . . . or undone, I should say.

"Open the fucking door!" he screamed again.

I was shaking all over now. From the sound of his voice, I could tell he wasn't fucking around.

"Shit!" I whispered as I slung my bag of money over my shoulder and thought about my escape. I whirled around aimlessly but soon realized that my Plan B didn't include Duke being at the front door of his fifth-floor condo. There was nowhere for me to go. It was only one way in and one way out and I damn sure wasn't jumping off the balcony. If it was the second floor, maybe I would've taken a chance, but I wasn't trying to die.

"Fuck! Fuck! Fuck!" I cursed as I saw my time running out. Duke was a six-foot-tall hunk of solid muscle. I knew I had no wins.

"Bitch! I'm about to take this fucking door down!" Duke screamed. This time I could hear him hitting the door hard. I couldn't tell if he was kicking the door or putting his shoulder into it. Although it was his condo, I had changed the locks to keep his ass out.

I spun around and around repeatedly, trying to get my thoughts together before the hinges gave in to his brute power. Hiding the money, I had stolen was paramount. My mind kept beating that thought in my head. I raced into the master bedroom and rushed into the walk-in closet. I began frantically snatching clothes off the hangers. I needed to use them to hide my bag of cash.

Wham!

"Oh my God!" I blurted out when I heard the front door slam open with a clang. I threw the bag onto the floor and covered it with piles of designer clothes. Things Duke and I had shopped for together when shit was good between us.

"Bitch, you thought I was playing with you?" Duke's powerful voice roared. "Didn't I tell you, you had to get the fuck out of my crib?"

He was up on me within seconds. I stood defenseless as he advanced on me so fast I didn't even have time to react. I threw my hands up, trying to shield myself from what I expected to come when he reached out for me. But I was too late. He grabbed me around my neck so hard and tight I could swear little pieces of my esophagus had crumbled.

"Duke, wait!" I said in a raspy voice as he squeezed my neck harder. I started scratching at his big hands trying to free myself, so I could breathe.

"What bitch? I told you if you ever fucked with me you wouldn't like it!" he snarled. Tears immediately rushed down my face as I fought for air. "Ain't no use in crying now. You should've thought 'bout that shit a long time ago."

Duke finally released me with a shove. I went stumbling back and fell on my ass so hard it started throbbing. I tried to scramble up off the floor, but before I could get my bearings, I felt his hands on me again. His strong hand was winding into my long hair.

"Ouch!" I wailed, bending my head to try to relieve some of the pressure he was putting on my head.

Duke yanked me up by my hair. Sharp, stabbing pains shot through my scalp.

"Owww!" I cried out as he wrung me around by my hair. I tried to put my small hands on top of his huge, animal hands, but it was no use. Hands I had once loved, I now despised and wished would just fall off.

"You thought it was all good right! You a fucking trifling ass bitch and I want you the fuck out of here!" Duke gritted. Then he lifted his free hand and slapped me across my face with all his might.

"Pl-pl-pl-please!" I begged him for mercy. But Duke hit me again.

I was crying hysterically. Partly from the pain of his abuse, but more so from our past. I would have never thought our relationship would come to this. It had been a long road, and all I wanted to do was teach him a lesson when I did the shit I did. I never thought I would have been facing this type of torment.

"I want all your shit out of here, you scandalous bitch! And don't take nothing that I fucking bought!" Duke roared, then he hit me again. This time I felt blood trickle from my nose. My ears were still ringing from the previous blow to my head. He hit me again. I was sure he had knocked one of my teeth loose.

"Yo Ak, get this bitch shit and throw it the fuck out," Duke called out to one of his boys. He never traveled anywhere alone. There were always two dudes with him at all times. The one I knew as Chris rushed into the closet and started scooping up my clothes and shoes.

"Wait!" I screamed, but it was for nothing.

"Shut the fuck up!" Duke screamed in response, slapping me again.

I could actually feel my eyes starting to swell. I finally gave up. My spirit was broken, and my body was sore. I watched as Chris and another one of Duke's boys slid back the glass balcony doors and started tossing all my shit over. I doubled over crying. More and more shit went over, and I was sure it was raining down on the beautifully manicured lawn below.

"Yeah . . . that's enough. Don't throw any of that jewelry or those furs outside. I got bitches I could give that shit too," Duke said maliciously. His words hurt. "A'ight bitch . . . ya time is up."

I shrunk back thinking he was going to hit me again. But he didn't. He grabbed me by the arm roughly. "Oww!" I cried out.

Duke was squeezing my arm so hard the pain was crazy. "Let's go," he said, pulling me towards the door.

"Nooooo!" I screamed, and then I dropped my body weight down towards the floor so he couldn't pull me.

"Oh bitch, you getting the fuck outta here," Duke roared. He bent down, hoisted me over his shoulder and started carrying me kicking and screaming towards the door.

"You can't do this to me! You will regret this Duke Carrington!!" I hollered.

"Fuck you!" he spat in return, opening the condo door and tossing me out into the hallway like a piece of discarded trash. I can't even describe the feeling that came over me. It was a mixture of hurt, shame, and embarrassment all rolled into one.

Duke slammed the door in my face, and I yelled for him to listen to me. My cries fell on deaf ears. My shoulders slumped down in defeat. Duke had left me in the hallway with no shoes, a short nightgown and nothing but my belongings on the lawn outside. I didn't even have the key to my BMW X6.

"Aggghhh!" I grunted in anger and frustration as I raked my hands through my tangled hair. I vowed from that minute on that Duke Carrington would learn just what all men have been saying for years . . . *it's cheaper to keep her.*

As I limped down the hallway of the building, all of the memories of how I had gotten to this point came rushing back.

CHAPTER 1—MAGIC CITY

One Year Earlier.

I walked into the *Magic City* and was immediately disgusted by the crowd that was already hanging around my post.

Same shit, different day, I thought to myself. I had been working at the well-known strip club for a minute, and it seemed like each passing month, more and more thirsty ass niggas showed up to spend their hard-earned money on a fantasy. I crinkled my face and looked at my watch just to make sure I had the right time. It was only eight-thirty in the evening and niggas were already starting to pack the club. I mean, damn, didn't they have wives at home giving them some ass. Maybe not, judging from how they came up in the *club* and made it rain almost every night.

I noticed a few of the regulars sitting around. Of course, the ones that were there early were the older, more broke niggas that wanted to take advantage of the specials. The ballers usually rolled in after midnight and when they did all the girls who worked at the *club* would put their best foot forward and try to get some of that baller dough.

I scanned the bar area and rolled my eyes as I headed for my post behind the bar. I wasn't no stripper chick. Bartending was my thing. I could mix the fuck out of a drink, but I wasn't about to shake my ass for dollars. I didn't know how the chicks up in the *Magic City* did it. Men touching them all over their bodies for as little as a single dollar bill. Hell Naw! Not me. All of those different hands all over my body, I would be sick after that shit. Then all that ass shaking, pole hopping and these chicks may or may not make a single dime. Not me, I needed guaranteed money. Even though these thirsty ass dudes didn't tip bartenders like they used to, they still wanted to sit up in my face and try to spit game my way. I probably turned down sixty niggas a night. I had so many of them telling me how beautiful I was. Yeah, yeah, I've heard it all. One nigga even told me I looked like Jada Pinkett Smith. Well, a few people told me that. Maybe it's true, maybe not. I did know that I was official. I kept my shit together: hair, nails, and clothes. Although money was definitely an issue, the package had to be presentable.

As a bartender, I had listened to every type of story about life there was, especially the same old story men told about their dry ass wives at home who didn't give up the pussy. Yada, yadda, yadda. All that said, bartending at the *club* paid the bills.

At least until a better opportunity came along, bartending was my gig.

I switched my ass past the early bird hounds who were already surrounding the bar trying to be the first to get their seats at the stage. It was Thursday, which meant, their favorite stripper was about to grace them with her presence.

Diamond was all the rage at the *Magic City,* and she was also my best friend and roommate. She had left for work before I did since she had to set up her look and her music. She was the club's Thursday night feature. A different stripper was featured each night of the week.

Needless to say, Thursdays were when the club was mostly packed. All the men loved Diamond. I mean, she was beautiful. She had a sweet baby face and the body of a video vixen.

I was almost to my post behind the bar when I felt a presence. I jumped.

"It's about damn time you showed the hell up!" I heard the voice and then felt somebody grab my arm.

"What the—" My statement was cut off. I was a bit thrown off.

"Lynise . . . I need a big favor," Diamond said in a pleading voice. Her words rushed out of her mouth like running water. She looked as if she had seen a damn ghost.

"Damn girl, you scared me grabbing on me like that," I huffed, looking at Diamond as if she was crazy. "What's the matter with you?" I asked confused.

"I need to borrow some cash quick before Neeko gets here. I ain't got the money to pay for my sets tonight," Diamond said, with urgency in her voice. She was rubbing her arms fanatically. The nervousness was written all over her face. I hated when she acted spooked, and it had been happening more often lately. I sucked my teeth at her.

"Why you need to borrow money Diamond? Didn't you do a couple of sets last night? I saw niggas making it rain all around you," I said, frustrated. There was no reason Diamond didn't have any money when I was sure she had probably made over five hundred dollars just the night before.

"I know, but I had to loan some to Brian," Diamond replied.

I threw my hands up in her face. I already knew she had given her no-good ass, wanna-be hustler boyfriend her money. I despised Diamond's boyfriend, Brian, but I tried to stay out of her business. He looked and acted like a buster if you asked me. However, Diamond was madly in love with his raggedy ass. He always had his hand out. I told her a million times it was supposed to be the other way around. Brian should've been taking care of her and trying to get her the hell up out of the *Magic City.* That's the way I saw it anyway.

But there was no turning Diamond against the slouch.

"How the fuck you keep giving that nigga all your money?" I barked at her. "He is a grown ass, able-bodied man! If he can't hustle up money or go get a damn job, then you need to leave his ass! You a sucka for love or what?" I was fed up with Brian or better yet, I was fed up with Diamond falling for his shit. He was always at our apartment, eating up our food and never lifting a finger or putting a dime in the pot.

Diamond put her head down and wore a sad frown when I told her about herself and her man. I knew I had hurt her feelings and I was immediately sorry. I loved Diamond. She was my road dog. We had been through hell and back together. Neither one of us came from good homes, and we had been down for each other for years. I just wanted her to make better decisions and be smarter with her money. I guess I should have been a little more sensitive. But I was too mad to be nice.

"Lynise, I wouldn't ask you if I didn't really need this," Diamond said somberly, shifting her weight from one foot to the other as if she had ants in her damn pants. I noticed she was fidgety as hell.

"Yo, this is the last time I'm loaning you money Diamond. We both struggling to pay rent and bills, remember?" I chastised her, taking my bag off my shoulder and placing it on a barstool so I could get my wallet. I dug into my purse and handed her a hundred dollars. That was enough for her to pay Neeko so she could do a few sets and make some money. That would lead to more sets. I knew she hated doing lap dances, but I was sure she would be doing some tonight to get some extra money. It was part of the *game.* And as much as we hated it, sometimes the *game* ruled us.

Diamond smiled and snatched the money from my hand. Then she threw her arms around my neck and hugged me. “Thanks, girl, you’re a lifesaver, that’s why I love you,” Diamond said, all of a sudden in a cheery mood.

“Just go knock them dead tonight bitch, ‘cause we need to eat dammit,” I said jokingly. Diamond smiled. She was so pretty when she smiled. I smiled back. I really loved my best friend. I watched as she trotted off to go get dressed for her sets. I shook my head as she finally disappeared down the steps to the Magic City’s dressing rooms.

“That damn girl gon’ drive my ass crazy,” I mumbled.

I still didn’t see how she thought this stripping shit was the best thing. The strippers at the *club* had to give Neeko, the club owner, twenty dollars for each set just to let them dance in his club. Then they had to pay the DJ twenty-five dollars for each set to play their theme music. Diamond told me on a good night she usually picked up around two hundred each set. To her, that made it worth it.

I couldn’t help but think about the bad nights. To me, none of it was worth it. The idea of having hundreds, maybe thousands of strange hands all over my body freaked me out. It didn't seem to really bother Diamond. However, deep down inside I think she felt just like I did about stripping.

One night, I watched from behind the bar as Diamond did her set. She got on her back at the edge of the stage, opened her legs like a scissor and spread her pussy lips open for a bunch of dudes sitting in the front row. I think she was just expecting them to throw dollars at her like usual. But I watched in horror as an old ass man, who I knew had no teeth, got up and actually put his mouth right on Diamond's spread eagle pussy and started slurping on her flesh. She definitely wasn't expecting it. The shock on her face spoke volumes. Diamond slammed her legs closed, smashing the man's head and he immediately jumped up. The man was smiling and wiping his lips. I thought I would throw up. Diamond looked horrified as she scrambled to her feet. The crowd of men bursts into cheers and money flew everywhere. Although I could tell Diamond was disgusted, she stayed up there and picked up every dollar.

That night, as we drove to our apartment, neither one of us said a word about the incident. Once we got inside, I heard Diamond crying in the bathroom as she took a scalding hot shower. That's when I knew I would never, ever, strip for anyone.

I was four hours into my shift, and I still had only made sixty dollars in tips. Talk about a slow ass night. I looked at the little chump change and sucked my teeth. Then just when I thought my night couldn't get any worse, in walks Devin, my sorry ass ex. I acted like I didn't see his ass at first, but he wasn't hard to miss.

"Wassup, Nini? You ready to take me back?" Devin said with a big smile on his face as he slid onto a barstool where I was mixing a drink for another one of the Magic City's regulars. I sucked my teeth and rolled my eyes at him. I slid the drink to my customer and rolled my eyes at the one dollar tip the cheap son-of-a-bitch placed on the bar. Devin noticed my disgust at the measly tip, and of course, he couldn't leave well enough alone.

"See if you were still with a nigga like me you wouldn't have to accept those penny ass tips," Devin said, flashing his perfect smile. Although I couldn't stand his ass for what he had done to me, he was still fine as hell.

"If you could keep your dick in your pants, maybe I would still be with you," I retorted, folding my arms across my chest.

"C'mon baby, you met me in a fucking strip club . . . did you really think I could control that," Devin said snidely. I swear I could've slapped the living shit out of him. All my thoughts of finding him fucking one of the white strippers in the club's champagne room came flooding back. The nerve of that muthafucka! While I was right outside at the bar working, he was fucking this bitch.

One of the other girls had come and told me I needed to go into the back and check things out. Initially, I was hesitant, but she insisted. When I found Devin and that bitch, I went off. I hit him in the head with a Heineken bottle, and I tried to rip that bitch's hair extensions from her scalp. Neeko almost tossed my ass out in the street over that shit. My forgiveness was paying for a couple of broken mirrors and tables. From that day forward, I vowed never to fuck with any of the club's patrons. Devin had taught me a valuable lesson. If a nigga is in a strip club, he ain't gon' be faithful for shit.

"You're a fucking animal. Get the fuck out of my face," I spat in response to his snide comment. I turned my back to him and went about my work.

"A'ight, suit yourself. When you ready to get out the hood, holla at ya boy," he said. Then he slammed a fifty-dollar bill on the bar. As bad as I needed that fucking money, my pride wouldn't let me take it. I snatched it up, crumpled it into a ball and threw it at him.

"Don't ever leave no money on this fucking bar unless you're buying a drink!" I screamed in a pissed off state over the music. "I don't need or want shit you got, you fucking pencil dick asshole!" That asshole just laughed. But I was seething inside.

My anger was overcome by the sound of Diamond's theme music. I immediately forgot about that fucking idiot, Devin, and turned to see my girl do her thing.

Diamond looked stunning in her all-white corset and thong set. She had feathers in her hair, and her make-up made her look like an angel. I watched her jump up on that pole with the skill of a gymnast. She twirled around it, letting her long, dancer's legs sway through the air artistically. Once she slid down to the floor, Diamond did a full split and with one pull of a trick string her corset flew off. The men in the crowd went crazy when Diamond's perfect C cup breasts flew free. She lifted one of her perky breasts and stuck her long tongue out and licked her own nipple. That was it. More cheers erupted from the crowd, and once again, more money flew.

I couldn't front, the woman was damn good at what she did. She knew how to work her body and work the crowd. She continued her dance until she was completely naked. Then out the corner of my eye, I saw Brian walk into the club.

"Shit!" I grumbled.

Brian never came to the club. He knew what Diamond did for a living and had agreed to stay away. I was instantly on high alert when I saw him. He was looking around with a crazed look in his eyes.

"Awww shit," I whispered to myself. I saw Brian walking towards the stage. I started to make my way from behind the bar. Diamond was making her booty clap, and a few of her regulars were slapping her butt cheeks and putting money in her ass crack.

Before I could make it to Brian's location or the stage, he had rushed to the edge of the stage. He grabbed one of the customers that had his hands on Diamond's ass and punched the man in his face. Screams erupted, and the DJ started yelling on the microphone for security.

"Brian!" Diamond screeched when she noticed what was going on.

The crazy muthafucka was outnumbered. All the guys in the front were together. Brian had just punched their boy. It was only a matter of seconds before the entire group jumped him. They had him on the floor punching and kicking him. Bottles were flying; chairs were being turned over. Then other niggas in the club just started going in on each other. Sheer pandemonium broke out. What the fuck? Did they think this was a John Wayne fucking western or what?

The security guards were truly overwhelmed, and they couldn't get a handle on all of the chaos. It wasn't until the DJ screamed that the police were on their way that everybody started to scatter. When the raucous group of guys jetted from the *club,* Brian was left in a bloody heap on the floor.

"Get him the fuck out of here!" Neeko screamed. Security came to hoist Brian's battered body off the floor.

Diamond ran to his side. "Brian! Please wake up!" she cried out. She grabbed his battered head, and his bloody skull covered her breasts. It looked like something straight out of a horror movie.

"This your man? Well, you can get the fuck outta here with him," Neeko boomed at Diamond. Security put both Diamond and Brian out. I rushed downstairs and grabbed Diamond's bag with her clothes. When I got outside, I helped her get dressed. When the ambulance got there, they put Brian in the back and Diamond climbed in with him. I watched as it pulled off. I covered my eyes with my hands. I had to get my thoughts together.

Finally, I turned towards the club and stared at the glowing sign that was in the shape of a stiletto heel. I shook my head, knowing I had to go back inside to get my things and my money. It was like my feet were cemented to the ground. That was how much I didn't want to go back into the club. I was so tired of working there. The whole club scene was taking its toll on me physically and emotionally. I stood outside as if I was standing at the gates of hell, waiting for the Devil to eat me alive.

The building I stood outside, looking at with disdain, was the hell I wanted to escape. It was my albatross. There was always something, and I was growing very weary of the entire scene. It took some time to get my feet to move, but I was able to walk through the club doors to collect my stuff. I walked slowly and deliberately as I headed back towards the bar. I could see the trail of Brian's blood from the stage leading to the exit doors. Neeko was clapping his hands and having people clean up the mess.

"It's back to business up in here! One dead monkey doesn't stop the show! We got ass to shake and pussy to show!" Neeko was calling out as he rallied the other strippers and his little crew to get the club back up and running.

I was disgusted with the whole scene. I was amazed at Neeko's lack of remorse or compassion. I rolled my eyes and bent down behind the bar to retrieve my money. It was my secret stash. Money I skimmed from the drinks I sold all night. That was the only way I could survive these days. I hurriedly stashed the money in my shoe and stood up.

I watched Neeko in disgust. He was acting like nothing had happened. "And tell your friend she is fired!" Neeko yelled at me.

"Oh please, Neeko . . . without Diamond's ass, this fucking club ain't gon' bring in no money, so I don't know who you are fronting for," I spat back at his greasy ass.

Neeko paused and thought to himself. He knew I was absolutely right. There wasn't no way he was going to take a chance and let Diamond go work at one of the other competing clubs in the Tidewater area.

"Yeah, I thought that would shut you up. You will see Diamond's ass right up in here tomorrow night, so stop the yip yapping," I said sarcastically.

Neeko started yelling at the other girls. He knew better than to say anything else to me. I gathered my shit.

"I have to find a way to get the fuck out of this shit," I told myself.

I meant every word too.

I needed a way out, and it had to be sooner . . . than later.

**THE END OF PREVIEW-
IN STORES NOW...**